ONCE UPON A TIME
IN THE NORTH

ONCE UPON A TIME
IN THE NORTH

Philip Pullman

Engravings by John Lawrence

DOUBLEDAY

DOUBLEDAY

UK | USA | Canada | Ireland | Australia
India | New Zealand | South Africa

Doubleday is part of the Penguin Random House group of companies
whose addresses can be found at global.penguinrandomhouse.com.

www.penguin.co.uk   www.puffin.co.uk   www.ladybird.co.uk

First published in Great Britain by David Fickling Books 2008
This edition published by Doubleday 2018

001

Text copyright © Philip Pullman, 2008
Illustrations copyright © John Lawrence, 2008
Design copyright © Together Design Ltd, 2008
based on a concept by Trickett & Webb Ltd

Typeset in 10pt New Baskerville
Printed and bound in Great Britain by Clays Ltd, Elcograf S.p.A.

A CIP catalogue record for this book is available from the British Library

ISBN: 978–0–857–53566–5

All correspondence to
Doubleday, Penguin Random House Children's
80 Strand, London WC2R 0RL

MIX
Paper from
responsible sources
FSC® C018179

Penguin Random House is committed to a
sustainable future for our business, our readers
and our planet. This book is made from Forest
Stewardship Council® certified paper.

Once Upon a Time
in the North

The battered cargo balloon came in out of a rainstorm over the White Sea, losing height rapidly and swaying in the strong north-west wind as the pilot trimmed the vanes and tried to adjust the gas-valve. The pilot was a lean young man with a large hat, a laconic disposition, and a thin moustache, and at present he was making for the Barents Sea Company Depot, whose location was marked on a torn scrap of paper pinned to the binnacle of the gondola. He could see the depot spread out around the little harbour ahead – a cluster of administrative buildings, a hangar, a warehouse, workshops, gas storage tanks and the associated machinery; it was all approaching fast, and he had to make quick adjustments to everything he could control in order to avoid the hangar roof and make for the open space beyond the warehouse.

The gas-valve was stuck. It needed a wrench, but the only tool to hand was a dirty old revolver, which the pilot hauled from the holster at his waist and used to bang the valve till it loosened all at once, releasing more gas than he really wanted. The balloon sagged and drooped suddenly, and plunged downwards, scattering a group of men clustered around a broken tractor. The

1

gondola smashed into the hard ground, and bounced and dragged behind the emptying balloon across the open space until it finally came to rest only feet away from a gas storage tank.

The pilot gingerly untangled his fingers from the rope he'd been holding on to, worked out which way up he was, shifted the tool box off his legs, wiped the oily water out of his eyes, and hauled himself upright.

'Well, Hester, looks like we're getting the hang of this,' he said. His dæmon, who looked like a small sardonic jackrabbit, flicked her ears as she clambered out of the tangle of tools, cold-weather clothing, broken instruments, and rope. Everything was saturated.

'My feelings are too deep to express, Lee,' she said.

Lee found his hat and emptied the rainwater out of it before settling it on his head. Then he became aware of the audience: the men by the tractor, two workers at the gas plant, one clasping his hands to his head after the near escape, and a shirtsleeved clerk from the administrative building, gaping in the open doorway.

Lee gave them a cheerful wave and turned back to make the balloon safe. He was proud of this balloon. He'd won it in a poker game six months before, in Texas. He was twenty-four, ready for adventure, and happy to go wherever the winds took him. He'd better be, as Hester reminded him; he wasn't going to go anywhere else.

Blown by the winds of chance, then, and very slightly aided by the first half of a tattered book called *The Elements of Aerial Navigation*, which his opponent in

2

the poker game had thrown in free (the second half was missing), he had drifted into the Arctic, stopping wherever he could find work, and eventually landed on this island. Novy Odense looked like a place where there was work to be done, and Lee's pockets were well nigh empty.

He worked for an hour or two to make everything secure and then, assuming the nonchalance proper to a prince of the air, he sauntered over to the administrative building to pay for the storage of the balloon.

'You come here for the oil?' said the clerk behind the counter.

'He came here for flying lessons,' said a man sitting by the stove drinking coffee.

'Oh, yeah,' said the clerk. 'We saw you land. Impressive.'

'What kind of oil would that be?' said Lee.

'Ah,' said the clerk, winking, 'all right, you're kidding. I got it. You heard nothing from me about any oil rush. I could tell you were a roughneck, but I won't say a word. You working for Larsen Manganese?'

'I'm an aeronaut,' said Lee. 'That's why I have a balloon. You going to give me a receipt for that?'

'Here,' said the clerk, stamping it and handing it over.

Lee tucked it into his waistcoat pocket and said, 'What's Larsen Manganese?'

'Big rich mining company. You rich?'

'Does it look like it?'

'No.'

'Well, you got that right,' said Lee. 'Anything else I got to do before I go and spend all my money?'

'Customs,' said the clerk. 'Over by the main gate.'

Lee found the Customs and Revenue office easily enough, and filled in a form under the instructions of a stern young officer.

'I see you have a gun,' the officer said.

'Is that against the law?'

'No. Are you working for Larsen Manganese?'

'I only been here five minutes and already two people asked me that. I never heard of Larsen Manganese before I landed here.'

'Lucky,' said the Customs officer. 'Open your kitbag, please.'

Lee offered it and its meagre contents for inspection. It took about five seconds.

'Thank you, Mr Scoresby,' said the officer. 'It would be a good idea to remember that the only legitimate agency of the law here on Novy Odense is the Office of Customs and Revenue. There is no police force. That means that if anyone transgresses the law, we deal with it, and let me assure you that we do so without hesitation.'

'Glad to hear it,' said Lee. 'Give me a law-abiding place any day.'

He swung his kitbag over his shoulder and set out for the town. It was late spring, and the snow was dirty and the road pitted with potholes. The buildings in the town were mostly of wood, which must have been imported, since few trees grew on the island. The only exceptions he could see were built of some dark stone that gave a dull disapproving air to the town centre: a glum-looking oratory dedicated to St Petronius, a town hall, and a bank. Despite the blustery wind, the town smelt richly of its industrial products: there were refineries for fish oil, seal oil, and rock oil, there was a tannery and a fish-pickling factory, and various effluvia from all of them assailed Lee's nose or stung his eyes as the wind brought their fragrance down the narrow streets.

The most interesting thing was the bears. The first time Lee saw one slouching casually out of an alley he could scarcely believe his eyes. Gigantic, ivory-furred, silent: the creature's expression was impossible to read, but there was no mistaking the immense power in those limbs, those claws, that air of inhuman self-possession. There were more of them further into town, gathered in small groups at street corners, sleeping in alleyways, and occasionally working: pulling a cart, or lifting blocks of stone on a building site.

The townspeople took no notice of them, except to avoid them on the pavement. They didn't look at them either, Lee noticed.

'They want to pretend they're not there,' said Hester.

For the most part, the bears ignored the people, but once or twice Lee saw a glance of sullen anger in a pair of small intense black eyes, or heard a low and quickly suppressed growl as a well-dressed woman stood expectantly waiting to be made way for. But both

bears and people stepped aside when a couple of men in a uniform of maroon came strolling down the centre of the pavement. They wore pistols and carried batons, and Lee supposed them to be Customs men.

All in all, the place was suffused with an air of tension and anxiety.

Lee was hungry, so he chose a cheap-looking bar and ordered vodka and some pickled fish. The place was crowded and the air was rank with smokeleaf, and unless they were unusually excitable in this town, there was something in the nature of a quarrel going on. Voices were raised in the corner of the room, someone was banging his fist on a table, and the bartender was watching closely, paying only just enough attention to his job to refill Lee's glass without being asked.

Lee knew that one sure way to get into trouble of

his own was to enquire too quickly into other people's. So he didn't give more than a swift glance at the area where the voices were raised, but he was curious too, and once he'd made a start on the pickled fish he said to the bartender:

'What's the discussion about over there?'

'That red-haired bastard van Breda can't set sail and leave. He's a Dutchman with a ship tied up in the harbour and they won't release his cargo from the warehouse. He's been driving everyone mad with his complaining. If he doesn't shut up soon I'm going to throw him out.'

'Oh,' said Lee. 'Why won't they release the cargo?'

'I don't know. Probably he hasn't paid the storage fee. Who cares?'

'Well,' said Lee, 'I guess he does.'

He turned round in a leisurely way and rested his elbows on the bar behind him. The man with the red hair was about fifty, stocky and high-coloured, and when one of the other men at the table tried to put a hand on his arm he shook it off violently, upsetting a glass. Seeing what he'd done, the Dutchman put both hands to his head in a gesture that looked more like despair than fury. Then he tried placating the man whose beer he'd spilt, but that went wrong too, and he banged both fists on the table and shouted through the hubbub.

'Such a frenzy!' said a voice beside Lee. 'He'll work himself into a heart attack, wouldn't you say?'

Lee turned to see a thin, hungry-looking man in a

7

faded black suit that was a little too big for him.

'Could be,' he said.

'Are you a stranger here, sir?'

'Just flew in.'

'An aeronaut! How exciting! Well, things are really looking up in Novy Odense. Stirring times!'

'I hear they've struck oil,' said Lee.

'Indeed. The town is positively palpitating with excitement. *And* there's to be an election for Mayor this very week. There hasn't been so much news in Novy Odense for years and years.'

'An election, eh? And who are the candidates?'

'The incumbent Mayor, who will not win, and a very able candidate called Ivan Dimitrovich Poliakov, who will. He is on the threshold of a great career. He will really put our little town on the map! He will use the mayoralty as the stepping stone to a seat in the Senate at Novgorod, and then, who knows? He will be able to take his anti-bear campaign all the way to the mainland. But you, sir,' he went on, 'what has inspired your visit to Novy Odense?'

'I'm looking for innocent employment. As you say, I'm an aeronaut by profession…'

He noticed the other man's glance, which had strayed to the belt under Lee's coat. In leaning back against the bar, Lee had let the coat fall away to reveal the pistol he kept at his waist, which an hour or two before had done duty as a hammer.

'And a man of war, I see,' said the other.

'Oh no. Every fight I've been in, I tried to run away

from. This is just a matter of personal decoration. Hell, I ain't even sure I know how to fire this, uh, what is it – revolvolator or something…'

'Ah, you're a man of wit as well!'

'Tell me something,' said Lee. 'Just now you mentioned an anti-bear campaign. Now I've just come here through the town, and I couldn't help noticing the bears. That's a curious thing to me, because I never seen creatures like that before. They just free to roam around as they please?'

The thin man picked up his empty glass and elaborately tried to drain it before setting it back down on the bar with a sigh.

'Oh, now let me fill that for you,' said Lee. 'It's warm work explaining things to a stranger. What are you drinking?'

The bartender produced a bottle of expensive cognac, to Lee's resigned amusement and a click of annoyance from Hester's throat.

'Very kind, sir, very kind,' said the thin man, whose butterfly-dæmon opened her resplendent wings once or twice on his shoulder. 'Allow me to introduce myself – Oskar Sigurdsson is my name – poet and journalist. And you, sir?'

'Lee Scoresby, aeronaut for hire.'

They shook hands.

'You were telling me about bears,' prompted Lee, after a look at his own glass, which was nearly empty and would have to remain so.

'Yes, indeed. Worthless vagrants. Bears these days

FINE SPECIAL OLD PALE

COGNAC

70% Proof

0128

MONTJULIEN

SHIPPED AND BOTTLED BY MATTEI BROTHERS, THORSHAVN.
PRODUCT OF FRANCE

are sadly fallen from what they were. Once they had a great culture, you know – brutal, of course, but noble in its own way. One admires the true savage, uncorrupted by softness and ease. Several of our great sagas recount the deeds of the bear-kings. I myself am working – have been for some time – on a poem in the old metres which will tell of the fall of Ragnar Lokisson, the last great king of Svalbard. I would be glad to recite it for you –'

'Nothing I'd like more,' said Lee hastily; 'I'm mighty partial to a good yarn. But maybe another time. Tell me about the bears I saw out in the streets.'

'Vagrants, as I say. Scavengers, drunkards, many of them. Degraded specimens every one. They steal, they drink, they lie and cheat –'

'They lie?'

'You can depend on it.'

'You mean they *speak*?'

'Oh, yes. You didn't know? They used to be fine craftsmen too – skilful workers in metal – but not this generation. All they can manage now is coarse welding, rough work of that kind. The armour they have now is crude, ugly –'

'*Armour?*'

'Not allowed to wear it in town, of course. They make it, you know, a piece at a time, as they grow older. By the time they're fully mature they have the full set. But as I say, it's rough, crude stuff, with none of the finesse of the great period. The fact is that nowadays they're merely parasites, the dregs of a dying race, and it would be better for us all if –'

He never finished his sentence, because at that point the bartender had had enough of the Dutchman's troubles, and came out from behind the bar with a heavy stick in his hand. Warned by the faces around him, the Captain stood up and half turned unsteadily, his face a dull red, his eyes glittering, and spread his hands; but the bartender raised his stick, and was about to bring it down when Lee moved.

He sprang between the two men, seized the Captain's wrists, and said, 'Now, Mr Bartender, you don't need to hit a man when he's drunk; there's a better way to deal with this kind of thing. Come on, Captain, there's fresh air outside. This place is bad for your complexion.'

'What the hell is this to do with you?' the bartender shouted.

'Why, I'm the Captain's guardian angel. You want to put that stick down?'

11

'I'll put it down on your goddamn head!'

Lee dropped the Captain's wrists and turned to face the bartender squarely.

'You try that, and see what happens next,' he said.

Silence in the bar; no one moved. Even the Captain only blinked and looked blurrily at the tense little stand-off in front of him. Lee was perfectly ready to fight, and the bartender could see it, and after a few moments he lowered the stick and growled sullenly, 'You too. Get out.'

'Just what me and the Captain had in mind,' Lee said. 'Now stand aside.'

He took the Captain's arm and guided the man out through the crowded bar-room. As the door swung shut behind them he heard the bartender call, 'And don't come back.'

The Captain swayed and leaned against the wall, and then blinked again and focused his eyes.

'Who are you?' he said, and then, 'No, I don't care who you are. Go to hell.'

He stumbled away. Lee watched him go, and scratched his head.

'We been here less than an hour,' said Hester, 'and you already got us thrown out of a bar.'

'Yep, another successful day. But damn, Hester, you don't hit a drunk man with a stick.'

'Find a bed, Lee. Keep still. Don't talk to anyone. Think good thoughts. Stay out of trouble.'

'That's a good idea,' said Lee.

A few enquiries brought him to a dingy boarding house near the harbour. He paid the landlady for a week's room and board and laid his kitbag on the bed before going out to seek a way of earning some money.

There was a brisk wind snapping in from the sea, and Lee pulled his coat around him and settled his hat more firmly on his head as he came out of a side street on to the harbour front. He found a line of shops facing the water – a ship's chandler, a clothing store and the like – and a dingy bar or two, and the broad, stone-built headquarters of the Provincial Customs and Revenue Authority, with a navy-and-white flag flying from the roof. From each end of this waterfront a quay stretched out ahead, forming a long sheltered harbour a hundred and fifty yards or so wide. At the far end stood a lighthouse on a headland that curved around from the right.

Lee looked at the boats in the harbour, taking stock. For a town in the throes of an oil rush, it didn't seem very busy. There was a coal tanker tied up at the quay on the right, sitting low in the water, so they hadn't unloaded her yet; and the only crane on that side was a big steam affair that was working to set a new mainmast in a barque, attended by more men than were necessary, each vividly expressing his point of view. It would take all day; the coal would have to wait.

On the other quay, to the left, there were two smaller anbaric cranes, the first busy loading barrels essential to take the greatest care with regard to the management of ballast. The balance between buoyancy and weight is a delicate one, and many an aeronaut, alarmed by the apparent reluctance of his craft to take to the air, has jettisoned too much lead shot too early, and as a consequence has had to let out gas to avoid soaring too high. It is a grave mistake to leave too little in reserve. A buoyancy of a very few pounds is quite sufficient to bear the largest balloon aloft. Patience and caution are the watchwords. Aerial navigation is no game for the reckless and improvident.

Notes to Chapter Six

1. As a matter of fact, this is impossible.
2. See *The Rapture of the Heights*, by Lt-Col Sir W.G. Hebblewhite, VC, CMG, FRAS.
3. These are normally made of whalebone.
4. The cubic capacity of a gondola is most commonly ascertained by Stirling's rule; but the following simple plan may be adopted for general purposes. Measure the length and breadth outside and depth inside. Multiply them together and by 0.6. The product is the capacity of the vessel in cubic feet.
5. Only a fool would suppose so.

Chapter VII

Procedure for Landing a Balloon

Figure 9.

⇡ = *force* ↑ = *velocity* ⇑ = *acceleration*

Mg is the combined weight of the balloon, occupants and ballast and needs to be carefully monitored.

R is resistance or buoyancy which will be affected by other factors like the height of the balloon, its velocity, air pressure, wind etc.

Size of resistance could be proportional to $\underline{V}$olume of balloon or to $\underline{V}$elocity.

If $R>Mg$ (Resistance greater than weight) then balloon will accelerate up. If $R<Mg$ balloon will decelerate, reach its highest point, then start descending. If too much gas is released the descent may happen too fast resulting in a crash landing. Extra ballast may need to be released to slow the descent.

Once aloft in the empyrean, with both gas and ballast in reserve, the aeronaut has little to fear. It is when he approaches the earth with a view to resuming his lowly status as a creature of gravity that the pilot of an aerial vessel encounters the first real danger of his flight. And yet by taking the simplest and most basic precautions, he may safely and easily negotiate the perils of landing, and emerge from his craft with all the nonchalance proper to a prince of the air.

The first and most essential matter to bear in mind is

of fish-oil into the hold of one small steam coaster, the second unloading the timber piled high on the deck of another. Beyond them lay a schooner, at which no activity of any sort was going on, and Lee guessed that to be the unfortunate Captain van Breda's vessel that couldn't load her cargo. Lee couldn't even see anyone on deck. The ship had a forlorn air.

Running along each quay was a line of stone-built warehouses, and at the near end of the left-hand quay was a cluster of offices including that of the Harbour Master. There was a pilot's launch tied up at the steps outside it, and a substantial steam tug a little further on; and if neither of those was busy, trade must be slow.

Lee rang the bell at the Harbour Master's office and went in, having read the brass plate beside the door.

'Good day to you, Mr Aagaard,' he said. 'I've come to see whether I can find any work around here. Scoresby is the name, and I have a cargo balloon in storage at the Barents Sea Company Depot. Any likelihood of an aeronaut's services being in demand, do you suppose?'

The Harbour Master was an elderly man with a sour and cautious expression. His cat-dæmon opened her eyes briefly and closed them again in disdain.

'Business is slow, Mr Scoresby,' said the old man. 'We have four vessels working in the harbour, and when they have gone, I do not expect any more trade for a week. Times are bad.'

'Four vessels?' said Lee. 'My eyes must be deceiving me. I saw five.'

'Four.'

'Then my eyes do need fixing. I saw a three-masted hallucination at the end of the east quay.'

'There is no work at the east quay, or at the west. Good day, Mr Scoresby.'

'And good day to you, sir.'

He and Hester left. Lee rubbed his jaw and looked left, along the quay, to the still schooner.

'I don't like to see any vessel so quiet,' he said. 'She looks like a ghost ship. There ought to be something the crew could be doing. Well, let's go and see what price they charge for hemp cord.'

He strolled along to the chandlery, where at least the stink of fish oil and tanning skins gave way to that of clean tarred rope. The man behind the counter was reading a newspaper, and he barely looked up when Lee came in.

'Good day,' said Lee, to no response.

He wandered about the shop, looking at everything, and as usual saw plenty he needed and little he could afford. He scratched his head at the prices until he remembered that this place was an ice-bound island for six months of the year, and everything had to be imported.

'How's the election going?' he said to the shopkeeper, nodding at his newspaper. 'Will Mr Poliakov become the new Mayor?'

'You want to buy something?'

'Maybe. Ain't seen anything I can afford, at your prices.'

'Well, I don't sell newspapers.'

'Then good day to you,' said Lee, and left.

He turned up into the town. The blue sky of morning had gone, and a bitter wind was bringing grey clouds scudding across from the north. There were only three people in sight: two women with shopping baskets and an old man with a stick. A group of bears stopped their rumbling conversation and watched him as he went past before beginning again, their voices so low he almost felt them through the soles of his feet.

'This is the bleakest, smelliest, most unfriendliest damn place we ever set foot in,' Lee said.

'I wouldn't argue with you, Lee.'

'Something'll turn up, though.'

But nothing turned up that afternoon.

The evening meal was served in the parlour of the boarding house, which was a dismal place with a small dining table, an iron stove, a shelf of religious books, and a small collection of battered and dusty board games with names like *Peril of the Pole*, *Flippety-Flop*, and *Animal Misfitz*. The meal itself consisted of a mutton stew and an apple pie. The pie was tolerable. Lee's fellow boarders were a photographer from Oslo, an official from the Institute of Economics in Novgorod, and a young lady called Miss Victoria Lund, who worked in the public library. She was as pretty as a picture, if it was a picture of a high-minded young woman of unyielding rectitude and severity. She was tall, and on the bony side of slim, and her fair hair was tightly pulled back into a bun. Her long-sleeved white blouse was buttoned to the neck. She was the first young woman Lee had spoken to for a month.

'So you're a librarian, Miss Lund? What kind of books do the people of Novy Odense like to read?'

'Various kinds.'

'I might look in myself tomorrow, see if I can find out some information. There's a book called *The Elements of Aerial Navigation* I'd really like to finish reading. Where is your library, Miss Lund?'

'In Aland Square.'

'Right. Aland Square. You been working there long?'

'No.'

'I see. So you're – ah – newly qualified, I guess?'

'Yes.'

'And...Is Novy Odense your home town?'

'No.'

'Then I guess we're both strangers here, huh?'

That brought no response, but her swallow-dæmon looked at Hester from the back of her chair, spread his wings wide, and then closed them again, followed by his eyes.

But Lee persevered.

'Would you care for some of this pie, Miss Lund?'

'Thank you.'

'You know, right after supper I thought I'd take a stroll along the waterfront and see what the enterprising citizens of Novy Odense have to offer in the way of night-time entertainment. I don't suppose you'd care to accompany me?'

'No, I would not.'

Miss Lund left the table immediately the meal was over, and as soon as she was gone the other two men laughed and clapped Lee on the shoulder.

'Fifteen!' said the photographer.

'I made it fourteen,' said the economist, 'but you win.'

'Fourteen what?' said Lee.

'Words you got out of her,' said the photographer. 'I bet you'd get more than ten, and Mikhail here said you wouldn't.'

'Careful, Lee,' murmured Hester.

'So you gentlemen are of a sporting persuasion?'

Lee said, taking no notice of her. 'Best thing I've encountered today. What do you say to a game of cards, now this delicious repast is but a fading memory and our fair companion has withdrawn? Unless you'd like to take a chance on *Flippety-Flop*?'

'Nothing would please me more,' said the photographer, 'but I have an appointment to take a portrait of the local headmaster and his family. I can't afford to miss it.'

'And as for me, I'm going to a meeting at the town hall,' said the other man. 'The mayoral election is hotting up. I need to see which way it's going to go.'

'Well, this is an exciting town, and no mistake,' said Lee. 'I can barely contain my exuberance.'

'Would you care to step along to the town hall and join me in the audience?' said the economist.

'I believe I would,' said Lee, and the other man's robin-dæmon twitched her tail.

The election meeting was certainly the place to be that evening. Men and women were making their way up the muddy street towards the town hall, which was brilliantly lit with gas lamps, Lee noticed with satisfaction: if there was a source of gas on the island, he'd be able to fill his balloon without too much difficulty – provided he could pay for it, of course. The people were dressed respectably, and so was Lee, to the extent of his one necktie; and they were talking with some animation.

'Is this the way they usually do politics on Novy Odense?' Lee said to his companion.

'There is a great deal at stake in this election,' said the economist, whose name, Lee had learned, was Mikhail Ivanovich Vassiliev. 'In fact it's the reason I'm here. My academy is very interested in this man Poliakov. He used to be a Senator, but he hates to be reminded of the fact. He had to resign over a financial scandal, and he's using this mayoral election as a way of rehabilitating himself.'

'Oh, is that so?' said Lee, watching the crowd on the steps, and noticing the uniformed stewards. 'I see there's a lot of Customs men around. Are they expecting a ruckus?'

'Customs men?'

'The bullies in the maroon uniforms.'

'Oh, they're not Customs. That's the security arm of Larsen Manganese.'

'I keep hearing that name…Who are they?'

'Very big mining corporation. If Poliakov gets in, they will prosper. Rumour has it that the company has been looking for a confrontation with the Customs; it's happening elsewhere throughout the north – private companies invading the public sphere. Security, they call it: what they mean is threat. I've heard they have a large gun that they're keeping secret, for example, and they'd love to provoke a riot and bring it into use – That gentleman is hailing you.'

They were at the top of the steps leading to the main doors, but they couldn't move any further because of the crush. Lee turned to look where Vassiliev was pointing, and saw the poet Oskar Sigurdsson waving and beckoning.

Lee waved back, but Sigurdsson beckoned even more urgently.

'Better go see what he wants,' he said, and made his way through the crowd.

Sigurdsson's butterfly-dæmon was fluttering round and round his head, and the poet was beaming with pleasure.

'Mr Scoresby! So glad to see you!' he said. 'Miss Poliakova, may I introduce Mr Scoresby, the celebrated aeronaut?'

'Celebrated, my tail,' muttered Hester, but the young lady at Sigurdsson's side had Lee's interest at once. She was about eighteen years old, and a contrast in every way to the starched Miss Lund: her cheeks were rosy, her eyes were large and black, her lips were soft and red, her hair was a mass of dark curls. Her dæmon was a mouse. Lee took her hand with pleasure.

'Delighted to make your acquaintance,' he said, and swept off his hat as well as he could in the crush.

Sigurdsson had been saying something.

'I beg your pardon, Mr Sigurdsson,' Lee said. 'I was unable to concentrate on your words because of Miss Poliakova's eyes. I wager you have dozens of young men come from all over the northlands to gaze at your eyes, Miss Poliakova.'

She let them fall for a moment, as if in modesty, and then gazed up through her lashes. Sigurdsson plucked at Lee's sleeve.

'Miss Poliakova is the daughter of the distinguished candidate for Mayor,' he said.

'Oh, is that right? Are we going to hear your father speak tonight, miss?'

'Yes,' she said, 'he will speak, I think.'

'Who is he up against in the election?'

'Oh, I don't know,' she said. 'I think two men, or perhaps one.'

Lee looked at her closely, while trying to muffle Hester's grumbling from inside his coat. Was this young lady genuinely slow-witted, or just pretending to be? She smiled again. She must be teasing. Good! If she wanted to play, Lee was in the mood for that.

The obstruction inside the door had been cleared, and the crowd was moving up the steps, marshalled by the Larsen Manganese security men. Miss Poliakova stumbled, and Lee offered his arm, which she took readily. Meanwhile Sigurdsson was pressing close at his other side, saying something that Lee couldn't quite hear and wasn't interested in, because the closer he got to Miss Poliakova, the more he was aware of the delicate floral scent she was wearing, or perhaps it was the fragrance of her hair, or perhaps it was just the sweet fact of her young body pressed against his side; anyway, Lee was intoxicated.

'What did you say?' he said to Sigurdsson, reluctantly.

The poet had been plucking at his other arm, and was eagerly gesturing for Lee to bend his head as if to receive a confidence.

'I said you might be able to make yourself useful to Olga's father,' Sigurdsson murmured as they entered the main hall. The place was set out with wooden chairs, and the platform was decorated with bunting and banners bearing the slogan POLIAKOV FOR PROGRESS AND JUSTICE.

'You don't say,' said Lee.

'I'll introduce you after the meeting.'

'Well…thanks.'

Lee's attitude to fathers was that he preferred to keep them at a distance. Fathers did not want their daughters doing what Lee had in mind. But before he could think of an excuse, he found himself in the front row, where all the seats were reserved.

'Oh, I can't sit here,' he protested. 'These seats are for important guests –'

'But you *are* an important guest!' said the poet roguishly, and the girl said, 'Oh, do stay, Mr Scoresby!'

'Damn fool,' muttered Hester, but only Lee heard her, as she intended.

They had hardly sat down when a stout official came out on to the stage and announced that they were closing the doors because the great desire of the people to hear the candidate speak meant that the hall was already full beyond its legal capacity, and they couldn't let anyone else in. Lee looked around and saw people standing three deep at the back and around the sides of the auditorium.

'He's a popular man, your father, no doubt about that,' he said to Miss Poliakova. 'What's his main policy?

What's he going to do when he gets into office?'

'Bears,' she said with a delicate shudder, and made a face expressive of polite horror.

'Oh, bears, eh,' said Lee. 'He doesn't like bears?'

'I'm scared of bears,' she said.

'Well, that's understandable. They're – uh – they're pretty big, after all. I ain't never dealt with your special Arctic bears, but I was chased by a grizzly once over in the Yukon.'

'Oh, how frightful! Did he catch you?'

And once again Lee felt as if he'd missed the bottom step in the dark: could she really be this stupid? Was she doing it on purpose?

'Well, he did,' he said, 'but it turned out the old feller only wanted to borrow a griddle to cook up a salmon he'd caught. I was agreeable to that, and we sat around yarning over supper. He drank my whisky and smoked my cigars, and we promised to keep in touch. But I lost his address.'

'Oh, that's a pity,' she said. 'But, you know…'

Lee scratched his head, but he didn't have to think of anything else to say because at that point a group of three men came on to the stage and the whole audience stood to applaud and cheer. Lee had to stand as well, or seem conspicuously rude, and he looked around for his boarding-house acquaintance, but among all the faces bright with fervour, the eyes ablaze with enthusiasm, he couldn't spot him anywhere.

As they sat down again Sigurdsson said, 'Wonderful response! Promises very well, wouldn't you say?'

'Never seen anything like it,' said Lee.

He settled back to listen to the speeches.

And very shortly afterwards, it seemed, he was woken up by a roar from the crowd. Cheers, clapping, shouts of acclamation echoed around the big wooden hall as Lee sat blinking and clapping with the rest.

On the platform stood Poliakov, black-coated, heavy-bearded, red-cheeked, with one fist on the lectern and the other clenched at his heart. His eyes glared out across the hall, and his dæmon, a kind of hawk that Lee didn't recognise, sat on the lectern and raised her wings till they were outspread.

Lee murmured to Hester, tucked into his coat,

'How long have I been asleep?'

'Ain't been counting.'

'Well, damnit, what's this diplomat been saying?'

'Ain't been listening.'

He stole a glance at Olga, and saw her settled, placid, adoring gaze rest on her father's face without any change of expression, even when the candidate suddenly banged the lectern with his fist and startled his own dæmon into taking to the air and wheeling around his head before settling on his shoulder – a fine effect, Lee thought, but Hester muttered, 'How long'd they spend practising that in front of a mirror?'

'Friends,' Poliakov cried. 'Friends and citizens, friends and human beings, I don't need to warn you about this insidious invasion. I don't *need* to warn you, because every drop of human blood in your human veins already warns you instinctively that there can be no friendship between humans and bears. And you know precisely what I mean by that, and you know why I have to speak in these terms. There *can* be no friendship,  there *should* be no friendship, and under my administration I promise you with my hand on my heart there *will* be no friendship with these inhuman and intolerable…'

The rest of the sentence was lost, as he intended it should be, in the clamour, the shouts and the whistles and the stamping that broke over it like a great wave.

The poet was on his feet, waving his hands above his head with excitement, and shouting, 'Yes! Yes! Yes!'

On Lee's other side, the candidate's daughter was clapping her hands like a little girl, stiff fingers all pointing in the same direction as she brought her palms together.

It seemed that the end of the speech had arrived, because Poliakov and his men were leaving the platform, and others were beginning to make their way along the rows of chairs, soliciting donations.

'Don't give that bastard a cent,' said Hester.

'Ain't got a cent to give,' muttered Lee.

'Wasn't that magnificent?' said Sigurdsson.

'Finest piece of oratorical flamboyancy I ever heard,' said Lee. 'A lot of it went over my head, on account of I don't know the local situation, but he knows how to preach, and that's a fact.'

'Come with me, and I shall introduce you. Mr Poliakov will be delighted to make your acquaintance –'

'Oh, no, no,' said Lee hastily. 'It wouldn't be right to waste the man's time when I ain't got a vote to give him.'

'Not at all! In fact I know he will be most gratified to meet you,' said Sigurdsson, lowering his voice confidentially and seizing Lee's elbow in a tight grip. 'There is a job he has in mind,' he murmured.

At the same moment, Olga clutched Lee's other sleeve.

'Mr Scoresby, do come and meet Papa!' she said, and her eyes were so wide and so candid, and her lips were so soft, and what with those eyes and those lips, and the delicate curls of hair, and that sweet heart-shaped face, Lee very nearly lost his presence of mind altogether and kissed her right there. What did it matter if she had the brain of a grape? It wasn't her brain Lee wanted to hold in his arms. Her body had its own kind of intelligence, just as his did, and their bodies had a great deal to say to each other. His head swam; he was fully persuaded.

'Lead me to him,' he said.

In the parlour behind the platform, Poliakov was standing at the centre of a group of men with glasses in their hands and cigars alight, and the little wood-panelled room was filled with laughter and the loud bray of congratulations.

As soon as Poliakov saw his daughter, he moved away from his companions and swept her into an embrace.

'Did you like your papa's speech, my little sweetmeat?' he said.

'It was wonderful, Papa! Everyone was thrilled!'

Lee looked around. On a table near the fireplace was a model of a strange-looking gun – a sort of mobile cannon on an armoured truck – and Lee was curious to look at it more closely, but the nearest man saw his gaze and swiftly covered the model with a baize cloth. It must be the gun Vassiliev had spoken of, Lee thought, and wished he hadn't made his interest so plain, for then he could have taken a longer look. But then he felt the poet's hand on his sleeve again, and turned to hear Sigurdsson's words to the candidate:

'Ivan Dimitrovich,' said the poet humbly, 'I wonder if I might introduce Mr Scoresby, from the nation of Texas?'

'Oh yes, Papa,' said Olga. 'Mr Scoresby was telling me about the horrid bears they have in his country…'

Poliakov patted his daughter's cheek, removed the cigar from his mouth, and shook Lee's hand in a bone-cracking grip. Lee saw it coming and responded in kind, and that contest ended even.

'Mr Scoresby,' said Poliakov, putting his arm around Lee's shoulder and drawing him aside, 'glad to meet you, glad indeed. My good friend Sigurdsson has told me all about you. You're a man who can see an opening – I can tell that. You're a man of action – I can see that. You're a shrewd judge – I can sense that. And if I'm not wrong, right now you're free enough to consider a proposition. Am I right?'

'Right in every detail, sir,' said Lee. 'What kind of a proposition might this be?'

'A man such as me,' the candidate explained, dropping his voice, 'finds himself placed in considerable danger from time to time. This is an excitable town, Mr Scoresby, a volatile and unpredictable environment for one who inspires the strong passions both of attraction and, I regret to say it, of resentment and dislike. Oh yes – there are some who fear and hate my principled stand on the bear question, for example. I need say no more about that,' he added, tapping his nose. 'I'm sure you understand what I mean. I will not be moved, but there are those who would like to move me, by force if necessary. And I am not afraid to meet force with force. You carry a weapon, Mr Scoresby. Are you willing to use it?'

'You mean you want to meet their force with my force?' said Lee. 'Glad to know you're not afraid to do that, Mr Poliakov. What's the job you have in mind?'

'There is a little situation at the harbour that needs resolving soon, and I think you are the man to do it.

You understand, there are things that an official body of men can do, and other things that need specialist work of a less public kind. There is a man who is trying to make away with a…with a piece of disputed property, and I want someone to stand guard over it, and prevent him.'

'Whose property is it?'

'As I say, it's disputed. That need not concern you. All you need to do is make sure it stays in the warehouse till the lawyers have done their work.'

'I see. And what will you pay?'

'You come straight to the point, my friend. Let me suggest –'

But before Lee could hear what Poliakov was going to offer, Hester gave a convulsive kick in his breast and said, 'Lee –'

Lee knew at once what she meant, and he looked where she was looking: past Poliakov, towards a

tall lean man lounging beside the fireplace, arms folded, one leg bent with the foot resting on the wall behind him. He was smoking a corncob pipe, and his dæmon, a rattlesnake, had draped herself around his neck and folded herself into a loose knot. His expression was unreadable, but his black eyes were staring straight at Lee.

'I see you already got yourself a gunfighter,' Lee said.

Poliakov threw a glance over his shoulder. 'You know Mr Morton?' he said.

'By reputation.'

'Let me introduce you. Mr Morton! Step over here, if you would.'

The man unfolded his long form from the wall and sauntered across without removing the pipe from his mouth. He was dressed elegantly: black coat, narrow trousers, high boots. Lee could see the outline of the guns at his hips.

'Mr Morton, this is our new associate, Mr Lee Scoresby. Mr Scoresby, Mr Pierre Morton.'

'Well, Mr Poliakov,' Lee said, ignoring Morton, 'I think you're making too much of an assumption. I've changed my mind. You couldn't pay me any money that would make me happy to associate with a man like this.'

'What's your name?' said Morton to Lee. 'I didn't catch it.'

His voice was deep and quiet. His snake-dæmon had raised her jewel-like head and was gazing intently at Hester. Lee rubbed Hester's head with his thumb and stared straight back at Morton.

'Scoresby is my name. Always has been. Last time I saw you, though, you weren't called Morton. You were using the name McConville.'

'I never seen you before.'

'Then I got keener eyesight than you do. You better not forget that.'

By this time every voice in the room was stilled,

every face turned to watch. The tension between the two men had silenced every other conversation, and Poliakov stood uncertain, his eyes flicking from one to the other, as if he were wondering how to reassert the dominance that had suddenly leaked away from him.

It was Olga who spoke first. She had been eating a small cake, and she hadn't noticed anything. She patted her lips and said as loudly as if everyone else was still talking, 'Do they have bears in your country, Mr Morton?'

Morton–McConville blinked at last and turned to face her. His dæmon kept her head fixed on Hester.

'Bears?' he said. 'Why, I believe they do, miss.'

'Horrid,' she said, with that childish shudder. 'Papa's going to get rid of all the bears.'

Poliakov shrugged his shoulders one at a time like a boxer loosening his muscles and moved forward a step to confront Lee directly.

'I think you had better leave, Scoresby,' he said.

'Just on my way, Senator. Happy to leave.'

'Don't call me by that title!'

'Oh, I beg your pardon. When I see a swaggering blowhard, I naturally assume he's a Senator. Easy mistake to make. Good evening, miss.'

Olga had by now realised that the atmosphere had changed, and her lovely dim face looked from Lee to her father and then to Morton and back to Lee. No one took any notice except Lee, who smiled with a pang of regret and turned away. But hers wasn't the last face he saw in the room, and neither was Morton's. Standing at the edge of the crowd was Oskar Sigurdsson, poet and journalist, and his expression was vivid with excitement and expectation.

'So we've decided what side we're on?' Hester said, back in the chilly little bedroom at the boarding house.

'Hell, Hester,' Lee said, flinging his hat into the corner of the room, 'why can't I keep my damn mouth shut?'

'No choice. That bastard knew exactly where we'd seen him before.'

'You reckon?'

'No doubt about it.'

Lee pulled off his boots and took the revolver out of the holster at his belt. He flicked the cylinder, found it too stiff to move, and shook his head in irritation: no oil. Since that soaking they'd had in the rainstorm he hadn't had occasion to use the weapon, except as a hammer, and the damn thing had seized tight. And here he was on an island that stank of every conceivable kind of oil, and he didn't have a drop to loosen it with.

He put the gun beside the bed and lay down to sleep, with Hester crouching restless on the pillow.

Pierre McConville was a hired killer with at least twenty murders to his name. Lee had come across him in the Dakota country. In the summer before he won his balloon in the poker game, Lee was working for a rancher called Lloyd, and there was a boundary dispute that erupted into a minor war, with half a dozen men killed before it was settled. In the course of it Mr Lloyd's enemy hired McConville to pick off Lloyd's men one by one. He had killed three men by the time the Rapid City gendarmes caught up with him. He shot two of the ranch hands from a distance, undetected, and then he made a mistake: he provoked a quarrel with young Jimmy Partlett, Lloyd's nephew, over cards and drink, and shot him dead in front of witnesses who could be relied on to testify that the dead man had started it. The mistake was that one of the witnesses changed his testimony, and told the truth.

McConville allowed himself to be arrested with the air of someone fulfilling a minor bureaucratic formality. He was tried for murder in front of a corrupted and terrified jury, and acquitted; following which he promptly shot the truthful witness dead in the street, with no attempt to hide what he was doing, as the gendarmes were riding out of town pleading urgent business in Rapid City. But that was another mistake. With the utmost reluctance the gendarmes turned round and arrested him again, after a brief exchange of lead projectiles, and this time set out to take him to the capital of the province. They never got there. In fact they were never seen again. It was assumed that McConville had somehow killed the officers and made off, and soon afterwards Mr Lloyd, sickened by the whole business, sold his ranch cheaply to the disputatious neighbour, and retired to Chicagoa.

Lee had appeared in the witness box during the trial, because he had been present when one of the ranch hands was killed, and he was asked to testify to the character of young Jimmy Partlett too. McConville's bony face and lean frame, his deep-set black eyes and giant hands, were unmistakable, and the way he stared across the court at the witnesses for the prosecution – with a measuring sort of look, a look of cold, slow, brutal calculation with nothing human in it at all – was unforgettable.

And now here he was on Novy Odense, guarding a politician, and Lee had been damn fool enough to provoke him.

In the middle of the night, Lee got up to visit the bathroom. As he felt his way down the corridor in the dark, wrapped in his long coat against the cold, Hester whispered, 'Lee – listen…'

He stood still. From behind the door on his left there came the sound of muffled, passionate sobbing.

'Miss Lund?' Lee whispered.

'That's her,' Hester said.

Lee didn't like to leave anyone in distress, but he considered it might distress her even more to know that her trouble had been overheard. He continued on his way, shivering, and then tiptoed back, hoping the floor wouldn't creak and disturb her.

But when he reached his door he heard the sound

of a handle turning behind him, and a narrow beam of candlelight shone into the corridor as a door opened.

He turned to see Miss Lund in a nightgown, her hair unpinned, her eyes red and her cheeks wet. Her expression was inscrutable.

'Apologies if I disturbed you, Miss Lund,' he said quietly. He looked down so as not to embarrass her.

'Mr Scoresby...Mr Scoresby, I hoped it was you. Forgive me, but may I ask for your advice?' she said, and then, awkwardly, 'There is no one else I can...I think you are a gentleman.'

Her voice was low – he'd forgotten that; and it was steady and sweet.

'Why, of course you may,' Lee said.

She bit her lip and looked up and down the empty corridor.

'Not here,' she said. 'Please could you...?'

She stood aside, opening her door further.

They were both speaking very quietly. Lee picked up Hester and entered the narrow bedroom. It was as cold as his, but it smelt of lavender rather than smokeleaf, and her clothes were neatly folded and hung instead of being strewn across the floor.

'How can I help you, miss?'

She put the candle on the mantelpiece over the empty grate, and closed the journal that lay next to the pen and bottle of ink on the little round table with the lace cloth on it. Then she pulled out the one chair for Lee to sit on.

He did so, still not wanting to look her in the face

in case she was embarrassed by her tears, but then he realised that if she had the courage to initiate this strange encounter, he should honour that by not patronising her. He lifted his head to look at her, tall and slender and still, with the dim light glittering on her cheeks.

Lee waited for her question. She seemed to be wondering how to frame it. Her hands were clasped in front of her mouth, and she was looking at the floor. Finally she said:

'There is something I have been asked to do, and I am afraid of saying yes in case it would be better to say no. I mean, not better for me, but better for – for the person who asked me. I am not very experienced in such matters, Mr Scoresby. I suppose few people are, before it happens. And I am alone here and there is no one to ask for advice. I am not putting this very well. I am so sorry to trouble you.'

'Don't apologise, Miss Lund. I don't know if I can give you advice that would be any good to you, but I'll sure try. Seems to me that this person who asked you to do something hopes you'll do it, or they wouldn't have asked. And…and it seems to me that the best judge of whether it would be good for them is them. I don't think you should worry yourself about giving a particular answer when that answer might suit your personal preference. It ain't dishonourable to consider your own interests. It might be more dishonourable to do what you think is the right thing for someone else when it ain't the right thing for you. This is about honour, ain't it?'

'Yes, it is.'

'Hard thing to get right.'

'That's why I asked for your advice.'

'Well, Miss Lund, if this is a thing you want to do…'

'I do very much.'

'And it won't harm anyone –'

'I thought it might harm…the person who asked me.'

'You must let them be the judge of that.'

'Yes, I see. Yes.'

'Then it would be honourable enough to do it.'

She stood still, this tall bony gawky girl in her white nightgown and her bare feet, her face so unguarded it was almost naked, a face where intelligence and honesty and shyness and courage and hope all blended into an expression that touched Lee's heart so strongly he all but fell in love with her there and then. He saw her soft hands holding her dæmon to her breast. And he saw her grace, the sweet overcoming of her young body's clumsiness – for she *was* young; and he thought how proud she would make any man who gained her approval; and he thought if once he was privileged to hold this treasure of a girl in his arms, he would never again look at a vapid doll like Miss Poliakova.

Suddenly she held out her hand to shake. He stood up and took it.

'I am most grateful,' she said.

'Happy to help, miss, and I wish you very well,' said Lee. 'I truly hope you can stop worrying about this.'

A few chilly seconds later he was in his own bed, with Hester beside him on the pillow.

'Well, Hester,' he said, 'what was that all about?'

'You don't know? She had a proposal of marriage, of course, you big fool.'

'She did? No kidding! How about that. And what did I advise her to do?'

'To say yes, of course.'

'Sheesh,' said Lee. 'I hope I got *that* right.'

Next morning Lee came down to a breakfast of greasy cheese and pickled fish, in the course of which each of the gentleman boarders took great pains to address the young librarian with careless charm, and she responded with silent disdain. Neither she nor Lee made any reference to what had happened in the night.

'A frosty character, our Miss Lund,' said the photographer when she'd left. 'She expects high standards of conversation.'

'She has a sweetheart in the Customs Office,' said Vassiliev. 'I saw them last night after the meeting. What happened to you, Mr Scoresby? Were you drawn into the maelstrom of politics?'

'Guess I was, for a minute,' said Lee. 'Then I came to my senses again. That Poliakov is a disapproving individual, and no mistake. Is he going to win this election?'

'Oh, yes. His only opponent is the present Mayor, who is an indolent and cowardly man. Yes, Poliakov will win, and then he will be perfectly placed to make a bid to return to the Senate at Novgorod. I fully expect to see more of him, unfortunately.'

'You know, I just remembered something,' Lee said. 'He began to mention a situation at the harbour that needed...whatever it was he said...resolving. Would that be the business of the Captain who can't load his cargo? Do you know anything about that?'

'Well, I don't know exactly what is going on down there, but no doubt our old friends Larsen Manganese have something to do with it. So Poliakov has a hand in it as well, does he? I'm sure that he will win that too.'

'Well now,' said Lee, 'would you care to make a little – ?'

Hester bit him quite hard on the wrist. Lee looked at her reproachfully.

'No betting,' she said.

'For shame!' he said. 'I was about to suggest to Mr Vassiliev that he might care to take a little trip down to the harbour to see what happens. Betting! Hester, Hester.'

'Unfortunately, I have other plans,' said Vassiliev. 'I have to inspect employment conditions at the tannery today, and then I must make my preparations to leave.'

'Well, enjoy the inspection, sir. If I don't see you again before you leave, I'll tell our fair companion that you took your broken heart away to nurse.'

It was a blustery morning, with little dashes of rain in between bright sunshine, and big white clouds hurrying across a brilliant blue sky.

'Pretty weather,' said Lee as they made their way to the harbour. 'Sooner be down here on the ground, though.'

'If you don't watch your step, you'll be under it,' said Hester.

Lee sat on a bollard at the water's edge and settled his hat lower over his eyes, because the glare off the water was surprising. He took out his little pair of field glasses and looked around the basin. The big steam crane on the right-hand quay had finished with the barque's new mast, and was now busy unloading the coal from the tanker into a train of rail wagons. As for the ships on the left, the one that had been taking on fish oil had done with that and was now loading what looked like bundles of skins, and the other vessel was riding much higher in the water after all her cargo of timber had been unloaded. Her decks were clear, and the crew were busy with scrubbing and painting. The only new vessel in sight was a dredger working near the harbour mouth, laboriously hauling up bucketfuls of sand and mud and dumping them into a lighter alongside.

On the schooner, nothing had changed. She lay still and silent at the quay. There was a knot of men gathered part-way along the quay at the corner of a warehouse, and Lee was about to train the field glasses on them when a harsh voice spoke behind him.

'What are you looking at?'

Lee put the glasses down carefully and turned round, taking his time. Hester moved a little closer. The man standing there was the red-haired Dutchman he'd helped out of the bar only the day before.

'Captain van Breda?' he said, standing up slowly and tipping his hat.

'That I am. Who are you?'

The man had no memory of him, which was hardly surprising, unless he was ashamed to admit it.

'The name's Scoresby, Captain. I was looking at that schooner, and thinking I wouldn't care to pay the harbour dues that must be piling up while she can't load her cargo.'

'You are an associate of that man Poliakov?' said van Breda, clenching his fists. His cheeks, under the red stubble, were suffused with a deeper crimson, and his eyes were bloodshot. It seemed as if he might fall to an apoplexy at any moment, Lee thought, looking at his dæmon – a big rough-haired mongrel bitch with a lot of wolf in her, her hackles raised, trembling and emitting a constant low growl. One or two passers-by glanced

at them curiously and walked on.

Not far away, a bear climbed up the steps from the water and shook himself, sending sheets of spray flying high in the air, before standing to look along the waterfront towards the two men.

'An associate?' Lee said carefully. 'No, sir. That's way wrong. I met the man last night at the town hall, and I told him I didn't care for the kind of man he employs. Anyway, I ain't got a vote in his election, and I fell asleep during his speech. Is that your ship?'

'Yes, goddamnit, and I don't like spies. What are you looking for? Hey?'

Hester moved a step or two closer and said a quiet word to van Breda's dæmon, who snapped and growled in reply. Hester turned to Lee and said:

'Lee, buy the Captain a drink.'

She was right: the man looked close to collapse.

'I'm no spy, Captain,' Lee said. 'Would you care to join me in a glass of hot rum? There's a bar right there. I'd like to hear about your situation.'

'Yes. Ja. Very well. Why not?' said the Captain, removing his cap and scratching his thick red hair with a trembling hand. All the brittle anger had left him, and he followed Lee helplessly into the bar.

They sat at a table in the window. Van Breda gazed obsessively out at the schooner, cradling his glass of rum while Lee lit a cigarillo so as to compete with the smoky stove nearby. Outside, Lee noticed the bear sit down near the bollard and then settle on his front, watchfully, great paws tucked under his chest.

'She's nearly lost to me now,' the Captain said.

'Your ship? Are you the owner as well as the skipper?'

'Not for long, if that man has his way.'

'How so?'

'Look at this,' said van Breda, and took a crumpled envelope from his pocket.

Lee drew out the letter inside. It carried the letterheading of the Novy Odense Harbour Company, and it said:

> *Dear Captain van Breda,*
> *In accordance with the Merchant Shipping Act*
> *II.303.(5), I am required to give you notice that unless*
> *the cargo currently stored in Number 5 East Warehouse*
> *is loaded by high tide on the morning of April 16, it*
> *will be impounded by the Harbour Authority and held*
> *for disposal by public auction.*
> *Yours truly,*
> *Johann Aagaard,*
> *Harbour Master*

'April the sixteenth,' said Lee. 'That's tomorrow. When's high tide?'

'Eleven thirty-two,' said van Breda. 'It's impossible. He knows it's impossible. He orders me to load my cargo, I want to load my cargo, but they refuse to open the bloody warehouse. They say I owe the Harbour Authority money. It's a goddamn lie. This is a concocted new charge that never existed before – they especially made it up to apply to this cargo. I ask for their authorisation for this new charge and they refer me to some goddamn law I never heard of. I know Poliakov is at the back of this. Him and Larsen Manganese. The Harbour Authority will impound my cargo and then Poliakov will bid for it at this goddamn auction, on behalf of Larsen, and no one will dare bid against him. Meanwhile I lose my ship. Who cares? Huh?'

'Let me get this clear,' said Lee. 'First they hit you with a new kind of charge for storing your cargo, and then they refuse to let you load it, and then they threaten to impound it if you don't?'

'That's it. They want to send me mad.'

'Why? What is this cargo?'

'Drilling machinery and rock samples.'

'Rock samples . . . Wait a minute. Would that have anything to do with oil?'

Van Breda dragged his gaze away from the schooner and looked at Lee directly for a moment.

'You're right. See, that's what it's all about, at bottom. Oil and money.'

'Who's the shipper?'

'An oil company from Bergen. See, I have the bill of lading...'

He fished another document out of his pocket.

'You sign the bill of lading before you load the cargo?'

'That's the system here. When the cargo is delivered to the warehouse it becomes the carrier's responsibility and the bill of lading is signed there and then. That's

BILL OF LADING

Bill of Lading Nº
76

EXPORTER Thorbjornsen & Co.

DATE 12 April 19

PORT OF UNLOADING **BERGEN**

CONSIGNEE	Shipper Certification		
L. Iversen, 24 Gjgaten, Bergen	J.F. Thorbjornsen		
	Carrier Certification Capt H van Breda "Mary Ann"		

Number of packages.	Kind of packages.	Weight.	Value.
8	3 wooden boxes mining equipt. 5 wooden boxes mineral samples.	6 tons	850 rouble

NOVY ODENSE PROVINCIAL CUSTOMS AND REVENUE AUTHORITY

the problem, see. I've already taken responsibility for this cargo, and I can't get the damn…can't even…'

He swallowed the rum convulsively.

'Why don't you talk to the Customs?' said Lee after a moment. 'I understand they're the law around here.'

'I tried. Not a Customs matter. All the Customs papers are in order. They wrote me a letter to say they're not concerned.'

'How long would it take to load?'

'A couple of hours. Not long.'

'And once it was on board, could you leave right away? Would you have to engage a tug, or a pilot?'

'No. I have an auxiliary engine, and enough fuel, and pilotage is not compulsory.'

'What about your crew?'

'All on board, but they won't be for long. They know the fix I'm in.'

'Because, you see,' said Lee, stubbing out his little black cigarillo, 'if you had the cover, you could take the cargo and run.'

Van Breda stared at him. He didn't seem to understand. His expression trembled between hope and despair.

'What are you saying?' he said.

'I'm saying I don't like Poliakov. I don't like the way he talks and I especially don't like the men he keeps company with. And I'm saying if you want to load that cargo, Captain, I'll stand guard for you while you do it. All you have to do is open the warehouse door.'

He pushed back his chair and went to the bar to

pay for their drinks.

A thought occurred to him and he said to the bartender, 'Say, do you know a man called Oskar Sigurdsson?'

'The journalist?' said the bartender. 'Ja, I know him. You a friend of his?'

'No. Just curious.'

'Then I tell you. He is poison. Pure poison.'

'Thanks,' said Lee.

He joined the Captain on the pavement outside.

He was about to turn towards the Harbour Master's office when he had a surprise. The bear by the bollard stood up, turned to them, and said:

'You.'

He was looking directly at Lee. His voice was profound. Lee felt himself startled witless for a moment, and then gathered himself and crossed the road to the waterside. Hester stayed very close to his feet, and Lee picked her up.

'You want me?' Lee said.

Face to face, the bear was formidable. He was young, as far as Lee could judge; his body was enormous, and his small black eyes quite unreadable. His ivory-coloured fur waved in ripples as the brisk wind played over it. Lee could feel Hester's little heart beating fast close to his.

The bear said, 'You gonna help him?' He looked briefly at the Captain, watching them from across the road, and then back at Lee.

'That's my intention,' said Lee carefully.

50

'Then I help you.'

'Do you know Captain van Breda then?'

'I know his enemy is my enemy.'

'Well then, Mr…Mr Bear –'

'Iorek Byrnison,' said the bear.

'York Burningson, the Captain needs to get at a cargo that's locked in the warehouse, and load it on his ship, and get away. And his enemy, who's my enemy too, as well as yours, wants to stop him. I reckon we got a short time to do it in, and then we're in trouble. Patience and caution are my watchwords, Mr Burningson, but sometimes we have to take a risk. You willing to risk trouble?'

'Yes.'

'Now I heard that your people make armour for themselves,' Lee said. 'Do you have armour?'

'A helmet. No more.'

The bear reached down past the edge of the stone wharf to the top of the flight of steps, and lifted up a battered, clumsy iron sheet of a curious shape and curvature. A chain hung from one corner, and Lee blinked with surprise as the bear deftly swung it over his head and hooked the chain from one corner to another under his throat. Suddenly the metal didn't look clumsy any more: it fitted him perfectly. The bear's black eyes glittered in the depths of the two great eye-holes.

Lee was aware that they were attracting attention. People were pointing, windows opening, and a little crowd of onlookers had gathered across the road. When Iorek Byrnison put the helmet on, there was an audible intake of breath, and Lee remembered the poet saying that the bears were not allowed to wear their armour in town.

The Captain joined them, looking at Lee questioningly.

'The odds just got better, Captain,' Lee said. 'This is York Burningson, and he's going to ride shotgun with us.'

'Byrnison,' said the bear.

'Byrnison. Beg your pardon. Now the first thing we have to do is get past the Harbour Master, so you leave the talking to me. Let's go down the quay, gentlemen, and open a warehouse.'

Lee led the way along the waterfront, and turned on to the quay itself. By this time the number of spectators had grown to thirty or so, and more were coming out from the side streets that led down to the harbour. They followed a short distance behind, pointing, talking excitedly, beckoning others to come and join them. Lee was aware of that, but not distracted: his eye was on the Harbour Master's office, where the door had opened briefly to let the man look out, and then closed again.

'You got that letter, Captain?' he said. 'Better let me have it.'

The Captain handed it over.

'Thanks. Now I'm going to be spinning a yarn, York Byrnison, so my attention will be kind of occupied, and I'd be obliged if you'd keep an eye out for any trouble.'

'I will,' said the bear.

They reached the building that housed the Harbour Master's office, and the door opened again. Mr Aagaard came out, fumbling with the last button of his uniform, and stood in the centre of the quay facing them.

'Good day, Mr Aagaard,' said Lee cheerfully. 'I hope this fine morning finds you well. Step aside, if you would, and Captain van Breda and my associate will go about our lawful business.'

'You have no business on this quay.'

'Oh, I don't think you're in a position to say that, sir. As an attorney-at-law I have every kind of business on this quay. My client –'

'Attorney? You are no attorney. You came to me yesterday claiming to be an aeronaut.'

'And so I am. As well. Now let me refer you to this letter, which my client has received from your office. Is this your signature?'

'Of course. What do you – ?'

'Well, Mr Aagaard,' said Lee, improvising happily, 'I think you should keep your law up to date. This letter is correct as far as the Merchant Shipping Act II.303.(5) is concerned, absolutely correct, sir, and I congratulate you on the terse and manly eloquence with which you have expressed this fragment of correspondence. However, let me remind you that a subsequent piece of legislation, the Carriage of Goods and Cargoes Act of 1911, Part 3, Subsection 4, Miscellaneous Provisions, specifically and by name supersedes the Merchant Shipping Act by stating that the right of a carrier to load his cargo once the bill of lading has been signed and countersigned, and I stress that, shall in no way be impeded, obstructed, or prevented by any provision of any previous Act, notwithstanding any local interpretations that shall be put in place. Now, Captain van Breda, have you such a bill of lading?'

'Yes, Mr Scoresby, I have.'

'And is it signed and countersigned?'

'It is.'

'Then, Mr Aagaard, I invite you to stand aside, sir, and let my client go about his lawful business.'

'I…this is not regular,' said the Harbour Master, whose cat-dæmon was scratching at his leg to be picked up. He bent stiffly and carried her to his breast, where she hid her face. He went on, 'I know nothing of these other laws, but Captain van Breda has not paid the duty on these articles, and –'

'Mr Harbour Master, just to save you any further trouble and embarrassment, I should remind you that the duty you refer to is a duty on importation and not on exportation, so in this case it doesn't apply. A simple and honest mistake for you to make. My client is willing to forgo any claims for compensation provided you release the goods at once from the warehouse. Furthermore, if it's a matter of duty payable and not a fee, as your own words before these fine and honest witnesses clearly indicated, then it's a Customs and Revenue matter, and the office of Customs is fully satisfied with Captain van Breda's right to move his cargo, and has no intention to levy any duty on it. Is that not so, Captain?'

'It is.'

'And do you have a letter to that effect?'

'Indeed I do.'

'Then there is no more to be said. Good day, Mr Aagaard, and we shall trouble you no further.'

'But…' the Harbour Master began unhappily, and then thought of something else. 'But that bear is wearing an illegal piece of armour, and he has no right to be on the quay.'

'A proper and reasonable response to unreasonable provocation, Mr Aagaard,' said Lee.

He stepped decisively forward, and the Harbour Master moved indecisively aside. The crowd had been still, trying to follow the arguments, and several of them looked less sure than they had been a minute before;

but Lee was more concerned about the little knot of men further along the quay. He knew the look of men like that.

'Nice piece of oratorical flamboyancy, Lee,' said Hester.

'Captain,' said Lee, 'you got any weapons on your ship?'

'I got one rifle. I never used it.'

'Ammunition?'

'Sure. But like I say, I never had to fire it.'

'You won't have to fire it. You bring me that rifle and I'll fire it if there's any firing to be done. Now if you began to load the cargo say within the next hour, could you leave with the tide like this?'

'The harbour is plenty deep. It will be fine.'

'That's good, because I might have to come with you. We both might. Now look out. These desperadoes are spoiling for an exchange of hot words. Say nothing and leave it to me. York Byrnison, once again I'd be obliged if you could cover the rear.'

The crowd had fallen back a little now, sensing that the mood of the events had changed, as Lee and the bear and the Captain walked on towards the five men who stood between them and the schooner. Hester was checking all around for other figures lurking in the alleys between the warehouses, or at a window above, or across the water on the west quay; for a handy shot with a good rifle could pick them off easily.

Lee was very conscious of the sound of their boots on the flagstoned quay, of the ceaseless scream of seagulls, of the chugging of the steam crane across the water and the clank and crash of the great bucket as it unloaded coal from the hold of the tanker and dumped it in the wagons. Every separate sound was bright and clear, and Lee and Hester both heard the little click at the same moment. It was the sound of a revolver being cocked, and it came from up ahead, Lee thought; but Hester's ears could pinpoint an ant on a blade of grass, and she said at once, 'Second man, Lee.'

The men were standing abreast in a line about fifteen yards ahead. Three of them were holding cudgels or sticks, but the other two had their hands behind their backs, and before Hester had finished saying 'Lee', Lee's pistol was in his hand and pointing straight at the second man from the left.

'You drop that gun right now,' Lee said. 'You just let go and let it fall behind you.'

The man had stiffened in surprise. He probably hadn't expected Lee to move so fast, and quite possibly no one had pointed a gun at him with intent before; he was just a boy no older than twenty. His eyes widened and he swallowed nervously before dropping the pistol.

'Now kick it over here,' Lee said.

The boy groped behind him with the toe of his boot and sent the pistol bouncing over the flagstones. The Captain bent to pick it up.

Then the man at the right of the line, the other man with his hands behind his back, did a stupid thing: he swung his right hand round and fired a shot from the big pistol he was holding.

But he didn't take time to aim properly, and the bullet went over Lee's head. The crowd behind screamed and scattered, but Lee had fired before the first cry arose, and his bullet caught the man's hip and spun him round so that he fell right at the edge of the quay, and then, unable to hold himself safe, he fell into the water, taking the gun with him. His cry was caught short by the splash.

Lee said to the other men, 'Now he's going to drown unless you pull him out. You don't want that on your conscience. Hurry up and do that, and get out of our way.'

He strode forward. The other men fell aside sullenly, and two of them slouched to the help of the man in the water, who was now splashing and shouting with pain and fear.

'Let me see that pistol, Captain,' said Lee, and the Captain handed it to him. It was a cheap and flimsy piece, and the barrel had bent when the boy dropped it. Anyone who fired it would be in danger of losing his hand. Lee tossed it into the water with regret, because he knew, in the moment he squeezed the trigger of his own revolver, that the cylinder had stuck for good. That was the one shot he was going to get.

'I'm going to need that rifle of yours real soon, Captain,' he said.

He put his gun back in the holster and looked around. The crowd behind was much bigger now, and the sounds had changed: across the water, the steam crane was still, the operator and the ship's crew staring across at the place where the shots had come from. In the absence of the clank and crash of the great bucket, Lee could hear the steady chugging of the dredger near the harbour mouth, and the excited murmur of the crowd behind.

The three of them moved on. They were not far from the schooner now, and Lee could see the crew gathered on the poop, watching wide-eyed as the little group made its way along the quay towards them.

But then one of them pointed at something back in the town, and the others shaded their eyes to look, and Hester said, 'Lee, you better look and see what's coming.'

By this time they were level with the stern of the ship, and opposite the last warehouse. A little alley ran between that and the one before it. Lee looked down the alley, looked up at the two rows of windows in the warehouse façade, looked across the harbour at the steam crane and the coal tanker, checking everything before looking back where Hester was indicating, and he noticed the bear doing the same.

'What the hell is that?' said the Captain hoarsely.

A large machine powered by some kind of gas-engine was making its way along the waterfront, and turning on to the quay. In the moment or two Lee saw it in profile he remembered the model he'd seen the night before in the parlour behind the stage at the town hall – the model of the gas-gun the Larsen Manganese people had been showing off. It was monstrous. The steel wheels and the half-track behind were grinding their way along the flagstones, and the crowd shrank back against the Harbour Master's office wall to make room for it.

'A gun?' said Iorek Byrnison.

'Yep,' said Lee.

'I do this.'

And the bear turned and ran silently into the alley.

'Captain, the rifle, if you please,' said Lee. 'Right now.'

'Oh ja. Ja. Mr Mate!' the Captain bellowed, and a voice from the rail called:

'Aye, skipper!'

'Mr Johnsen, would you go and bring my rifle and the box of ammunition from the lazaret, if you please. Look lively.'

Further down the quay, the gun had stopped. The crowd was backing away to give it room. A man in maroon stood beside it, and shouted something through a megaphone which was utterly incomprehensible. Lee spread his hands wide.

The man shouted again, and again it was impossible to understand him. Lee shook his head.

Someone ran down the gangplank behind him, and hurried up to the Captain. A moment later, van Breda handed the rifle to Lee.

'Oh, thank you, Captain. Well, my sweet Aunt Betsy! A Winchester! How about that?'

'You know this rifle?'

'Best there is. And in good order, too.'

He swiftly filled the magazine, cursing his

carelessness over the pistol, and enjoying the feel of a well-balanced and well-oiled piece of machinery. He felt much better having it in his hands.

'Captain,' he said, 'this is the warehouse, this one right here?'

'It is.'

'Do you know exactly where your cargo is stowed?'

'Yes. All we need to do is open the door.'

Lee took a handful of cartridges from the box and dropped them into his pocket, then turned to look back along the quay.

For the gas-gun had resumed its grinding forward movement, and Lee could see now how it was crewed: it looked like one man to drive it, two to fire and reload. The long barrel rose and swung from left to right and back again, before settling on the stern of the schooner.

It was a thing to smash down buildings with, a thing to sink a ship, and Lee thought that if they fired it just once it would be the end of this adventure, and the end of him, too.

It came closer, and Lee lifted the rifle to his shoulder. It was nearly at the end of the middle warehouse, just opposite the alley between that and the next to last, and Lee's finger tightened on the trigger –

But before anything else happened, there came a thunder of feet and a roar such as Lee had never heard, and out of the alley burst Iorek Byrnison, to hurl the huge weight of himself against the bulk of the gun.

Lee gave a cry of surprise – he couldn't help it.

The gunners cried out in alarm as the wheels and the track skidded and scraped on the stone. Iorek's first smash had swung the front of the gun round so that the barrel was pointing out over the harbour, and the driver desperately hauled at the brake; but then Iorek set his shoulder to the side of the carriage, and heaved and shoved until the two front wheels had rolled over the edge, and the whole gun tilted forwards. The gunners were shouting with alarm and struggling to swing the barrel back round, and then Iorek shoved again and the gun went off with a flash of fire and smoke and a deafening bang, sending a shell skipping across the water, right into the side of the quay beside the coal tanker. It exploded with a plume of water, and rock hurled high into the air, scattering the ship's crew and the crane driver. But few noticed them, because the blast of the gun had infuriated Iorek, and now he had his claws under the rear of the carriage, and while the engine roared and the caterpillar tracks screamed on the stone, the bear straightened his back with an immense effort and heaved the whole weapon and its three-man crew into the water with a huge splash. One of the men jumped clear; the other two disappeared with the gun.

Cheers from the ship's crew, a yell of delight from Lee.

The bear dropped to all fours again and sauntered along to join Lee at the schooner.

'Well, I'd hate to see you get angry, York Byrnison,' said Lee.

Across the water, the crew of the coal tanker were cautiously inspecting the damage to the wharf. The crane driver was shaking his head at the bosun, who was yelling at him to get back to work, and the driver in charge of the rail trucks was running back from the engine to see what had happened. Even the dredger had stopped work for a minute, but presently the steady chugging resumed.

For the moment, no one was moving among the crowd further down the quay. Lee looked around more carefully. To his right as he faced towards the town loomed the bulk of the warehouse: a three-storey building in grey stone, with a row of windows on the top and middle floors. The massive doors were of steel, and opened inwards. Projecting from the centre of the wall above the top floor, just under the eaves, was a beam and tackle for lifting goods directly up. The sun was bright now, for the clouds had blown away, and it shone full on the warehouse front from over Lee's left shoulder when he faced down the quay.

Behind him, the Captain was shouting orders, and Lee heard a muffled bang from below decks, followed by a coughing throb, which told of the detonator starting the heavy-oil engine. On the foredeck, two sailors were busily removing the cover from the forward hatch, while another man was checking the tackle on a derrick that had been rigged over it on the foremast.

Suddenly Hester said, 'Top floor right, Lee.'

He swung the rifle up towards the warehouse and saw what she'd seen: a flicker of movement behind the third window in from the end. He kept the rifle trained directly on it, but saw no more movement.

Iorek Byrnison stood beside Lee, glaring down the length of the quay towards the crowd. The Captain and the mate came down to join them.

'Now, Mr Mate,' said Lee, 'how you going to move that cargo of yours?'

'It's on trucks,' the mate said. 'We set it all up ready before they locked us out. It won't take half an hour.'

'Right. Captain, tell me this: what's the layout in the warehouse? What do we see when we open the door?'

'The space is fully open. There are columns, I don't know how many, stone columns supporting the floors above. On the ground floor at present there are mostly bundles of furs and skins. My cargo is near the far wall on the left-hand side, stacked ready on trucks.'

'These bundles of skins – how high are they stacked? Can I look right across the whole space in there, or are they too high to see over?'

'Too high, I think.'

'And what about stairs?'

'In the centre at the back.'

'And the upper floors?'

'I don't know what –'

'Lee! Top left!' said Hester, and in the same moment Lee caught a flash of sunlight as a window opened.

He swung the rifle up, and that must have put the sharp-shooter off, because the one snatched pistol shot went past him and thudded into the deck of the schooner. Lee fired back at once. The window shattered, scattering broken glass down three floors to the ground, but there was no sign of the gunman.

Iorek Byrnison looked up briefly, and then said, 'I open the door.'

Lee half expected to see him charge and flatten it in one rush, but the bear's behaviour was quite different: he touched the steel door several times in different places with a claw, tapping, pressing, touching with the utmost delicacy. He seemed to be listening to the sound it made, or feeling for some quality in the resistance it offered.

Lee and Hester were standing back from the building, at the edge of the quay, from which point he could see all the windows.

'Lee,' said Hester quietly, 'if that's McConville in there –'

'Ain't no if, Hester. I've known he was in there from the first.'

'Mr Scarsby,' said the bear, 'shoot a bullet at this spot.' He scratched an X at a point near the upper hinge of the right-hand door.

Lee looked up to make sure the gunman at the window was still out of sight, checked back along the quay to see the crowd hanging back still, unwilling to come closer just yet, checked with the Captain that the men were ready.

'Right,' he said. 'Now this is what we'll do. York Byrnison and I will open the door, and I'll go in first. There's a gunman in there – maybe more than one – and I want to make sure they're not intending any unpleasantness. If you take my advice, Mr Mate, you and your crew will wait on board and out of sight till you hear from me or York Byrnison that the place is safe.'

'You expecting more trouble?'

'Oh, I always expect trouble. York Byrnison, you ready?'

'Ready.'

'Here goes.'

He lifted the rifle, took aim at the X on the door, and fired. A neat hole appeared in the steel sheet, and that was all; but then Iorek Byrnison reached out a paw and pushed gently, and the entire door fell inwards with a deafening crash.

At once Lee leapt past Iorek and ran into the warehouse, making for the open staircase he could dimly see straight ahead.

And at the same moment a shot blazed out from dead ahead, somewhere in the ranks and rows of stinking bundles. The bullet clipped the shoulder of Lee's coat, feeling like the clutch of a ghost, and then came a cry and a crash from the ship outside. Lee stopped and took cover behind a row of bales. Stupid to rush in like that, he thought: after the bright sun on the quayside, this was almost like night, and his opponent's eyes were already well adjusted.

'Where is he?' came the bear's voice from behind him.

'He fired from dead ahead,' said Lee quietly. 'But there's at least one other man upstairs. If you take this one, I'll go on up and deal with him.'

As he said that, he heard another shot, and another, from above, and a cry of distress and alarm from the ship. Lee and Iorek ran at the same moment – Lee lightly for the stairs, with Hester bounding ahead, and Iorek slow and ponderous for the first two or three steps as he drove against the inertia of his great bulk, but once moving he was unstoppable. Lee, halfway up the open iron staircase, saw bales of fur and skins hurled aside like thistledown, and then came two or three quick shots and a scream of fear, suddenly cut short in a hideous grunt.

More shots from high up. Lee leapt up to the next floor, which was largely empty, with just a few wooden cases resting on pallets near the back wall; but it was much lighter here, with sunlight pouring in through the long line of windows.

And there was no one in sight.

Lee doubled back and made for the next flight of stairs. He couldn't run silently on these bare floors, and he knew that the man up there would hear him coming and have plenty of time to line up a shot towards the top of the stairs. He stopped just below the level of the upper floor, and raised his hat high on the rifle barrel, and at once a shot spun it round and round – a good shot, instant and accurate.

But it told him where the man was shooting from: the far corner, on the right as you looked at the warehouse from the quay. Lee stopped and considered.

What he didn't know was how clear the floor was, whether there were barrels or boxes for the other man to hide behind, or whether he would have a clear shot to the corner.

Nor did he know whether McConville was alone, or whether he had an accomplice who could shoot Lee in the back from the other corner. After all, the window that had opened when Lee was outside was on the left.

He looked at the staircase he was standing on. The steps were open iron-work, about ten feet wide, and they led up towards a landing at the back wall of the warehouse. His best chance was to take it at a run, hope to avoid any bullets, and shoot fast as soon as he could.

'Lee,' whispered Hester, 'pick me up.'

He bent to lift her. She wanted to listen, and the higher she was the better. She sat tensely in his arms, flicking her ears, and then whispered:

'There's two of 'em. One left, one right.'

'Just two?' he whispered back.

'There's something in the way – maybe barrels. Use that smokeleaf tin.'

He put her down and fished in his waistcoat pocket for the tin he kept his cigarillos in. He tipped the last three out and slipped the tin back, keeping the lid. He'd polished the inside to a bright gloss until it was almost as good as a mirror.

The floor above was a foot or so over his head: heavy pine boards, with an iron flange at the edge and a guardrail around the opening for the stairs.

Moving cautiously up to the next step and keeping his head low, Lee lifted the tin lid up very slowly close to the nearest stanchion of the rail, and tilted it so he saw along the floor and towards the right-hand corner, where the shot had come from. He could see no one, but that was because a row of heavy barrels stood in the way: two rows, in fact, one stacked on top of the other, separated by the pallets the barrels were standing on.

Lee knew well how small a movement would catch a watching eye, and taking infinite pains to move slowly, he turned the lid round to face the other corner. That side was empty, apart from some piece of machinery under a tarpaulin, and Lee could see the gunman clearly, standing behind it and looking over the top, with his rifle pointed just above where Lee was standing. It was not McConville.

The stone columns holding up the roof – sixteen of them, each about two feet in diameter – were equally spaced along the length of the room in two rows, one near the back wall and one near the front, and Lee calculated that if he could reach the column closest to the stairs on the gunman's side, he might be able to shelter behind it while dealing with him; but that still left McConville free to shoot him in the back. This was really a hopeless situation, and he shouldn't have got himself into it.

In fact, it was like pretty well every other situation he'd ever been in. And I'm still here, he thought, and Hester twitched her ears. He slipped the smokeleaf lid back into his pocket.

Then from down below there came the loud scraping clang of the big steel door being hauled out of the way, and under cover of the noise, Lee took a good grip of the rifle and launched himself upwards as fast as he could, running at an angle to the top of the steps and left along the floor to the shelter of the nearest column.

His ears were full of noise – shots from right and left, and the echoes from the bare stone walls. He reached the column and pressed himself behind it.

It was the third column from the end on that

side. The tarpaulin-covered machinery behind which the gunman was hiding was near the middle of the end wall, and it was a little less high than the head of a man, which meant the shooter had to crouch all the time: not a comfortable position to hold for long. The best way to deal with him, if he'd been alone, would be to wait till he  moved, as he'd have to eventually, and pick him off with one shot.

But behind Lee, at the far end of the warehouse, McConville had a better place of concealment and a clear line of fire. If he'd just had a pistol it wouldn't be so bad, but those sounded like rifle shots, and Lee, pressed against the column, felt as well as heard the bullets striking his narrow shelter. McConville wouldn't miss too many times with a rifle.

The first volley of shots came to an end.

Lee ran again, past the second column, on to the first – a little further from McConville, making it safer as the angle tightened; and closer to the other man, whose shoulder – was it? – Lee could see, imperfectly concealed.

He raised the rifle. In the same moment he pressed the trigger and McConville yelled, 'Duck!'

His bullet reached the man before the warning did,

and there was a grunt, a thud as he dropped his weapon, then a long withdrawn breath, and then silence.

Lee looked at the tarpaulin, and calculated: five running steps away, from right to left across McConville's line of sight, in about a second and a half. It should be possible.

And it was. McConville fired twice and missed, but Lee made it, and found the other gunman sprawled on his back with his pistol too far away to reach, and the eyes in his pale face burning. A pool of blood was spreading out around him like a great red wing unfurling. His cat-dæmon crouched by his side, trembling.

'You've done for me,' the gunman said in the voice of a ghost.

Lee said, 'Yep, you're bleeding a lot. Reckon I have. Is that McConville over there?'

'Morton. Ain't no McConville.'

'Wouldn't that be dandy. What's he carrying?'

'Go stick your head up your ass.'

'Oh, you're a nice man. Now hold your tongue.'

Keeping low, he patted the man's chest and sides to make sure he wasn't carrying another weapon, and then, ignoring him, turned his attention to the other end of the warehouse. In one way, it didn't matter if he and McConville stood and hid from each other all day long. Captain van Breda could load his cargo without being shot at, and get away with it. But sooner or later, either Lee or McConville was going to have to move, and the first one to do so would probably die.

Suddenly a fusillade of shots rang out, and bullets

thudded into the walls behind Lee and the tarpaulin-covered machinery in front. Two or three struck the columns, and whined off into the corners.

And in the middle of the barrage, Lee – who was crouching low behind the machinery – suddenly found himself knocked to the floor and dizzy with shock. Had he taken a bullet? Was he hurt? It was the strangest sensation – and then with a horrible lurch of nausea, he saw his Hester in the grasp of the fallen gunman's good hand. He had her around the throat. Lee was choking with her, but the outrage – a stranger's hand on his dæmon! – was worse.

He dragged his rifle round till the barrel was hard against the man's side, and shot him dead.

Hester leapt away and into Lee's arms, and he'd never felt her tremble so violently.

'All right, gal, it's over,' he whispered.

'It ain't,' she whispered. 'There's still McConville.'

'Think I'd forgot that, you dumb rabbit? Git a hold a yourself.'

He rubbed her ears with his thumb and put her down gently. Then he looked out again, very cautiously, along the line of columns to the stack of barrels at the other end of the empty floor. There was no movement.

But Lee realised with a little flicker of hope that McConville wasn't only brutal: he was stupid too. A clever man would have done nothing, held his fire, kept as still as a stone until Lee had either killed or been killed by the other man. If Lee came out on top he might have thought all the danger was gone, and

McConville could pick him off when his back was turned. Instead of that, what did the fool do but give himself away. So there might be a chance.

Those columns…Two rows of eight, equally spaced along the length of the building, back and front. When Lee looked past the left side of the row at the front, by the windows, he could see the whole room, almost, clear across the centre of the big floor to the stack of barrels; but when he looked past the right side of the columns, he could see nothing but the narrow passage between the front wall and the row of overlapping columns, right down to the side wall at the far end.

But that meant in turn that McConville would have the same view. If Lee moved along between the row of columns and the front wall, he'd be invisible to the other man for some of the way, at least.

It was the best chance he had. He looked down at Hester, and she flicked her ears: ready. Lee quickly filled the magazine of the Winchester (and what a sweet weapon this was) and set off, making as little noise as leather-shod feet could on a wooden floor.

For the first three or four columns he was safely invisible, and he was ready to snap a shot as soon as anything moved into sight at the other end. The further he got, though, the more dangerous, because as the angle increased so did the gaps between the columns.

Couldn't be helped. Take the rest at a run. He stopped at the last point where he was still fully concealed, opposite the big doors right in the centre that opened for goods to come up by the hoist, and then gripped the rifle and ran.

And in the same moment he thought, *My shadow – damn, he can see my shadow –*

The sun was pouring in through the windows. McConville had been able to follow his progress every step of the way; and no sooner had Lee realised that than two shots rang out, and he dropped. He was hit, but he had no idea where. He'd sprawled in the space between the second and third columns. With all his might he dragged himself up and flung himself forward towards the rack of barrels. If he was close against it on this side, McConville wouldn't be able to see him.

Maybe.

He made it, and slipped down to the floor. Hester was close by, trembling. Lee brought his finger to his lips, and he could do that because his hand was free, and his hand was free because he'd dropped the rifle.

It lay out in the open, several feet away and unreachable.

He sat there with his back to the lower rack of barrels, smelling the stinking fish oil, feeling his blood race, listening to every drip and creak and scrape and click, and holding back the pain that was prowling around just waiting to pounce.

It was his left shoulder, as he discovered a few moments later. Where exactly he didn't know, because the pain inconsiderately took up residence like a bully and demanded all the feeling there was; but Lee tried to move his left hand and arm and found them still working, though badly weakened, so he guessed

McConville's bullet hadn't found a bone.

Damn, there was blood all over the place. Where the hell was that coming from? Was he hit somewhere else as well?

He shook his head to clear it, and drops of blood flew off and  splashed across his face. Simultaneously his left ear felt as if a tiger had taken a bite out of it, and Lee had to hold his breath to avoid gasping. Well, ears did bleed, no doubt about it, and if it was no worse than that, then it was better than it might have been.

Silence in the warehouse, apart from the drip of blood on to the floor.

Outside, the distant sounds of work, and the cry of seagulls.

Lee sat, stiffening with pain, with one gun that didn't work and yards from another that did, in the deepening stench of fish oil. Somebody's bullet – probably his – had punctured one of the barrels, and not far away from where he'd fallen a steady trickle of the stuff was leaking down from the top rack and spreading slowly across the floor. In another five minutes he'd be sitting right in it.

Hester sat crouched tightly against his side. She was

hurt by his wounds, but she wouldn't complain.

'Scoresby,' came a voice from the other side of the rack of barrels.

Lee said nothing.

'I know you're there, you cheap son of a bitch, and I know I got you,' the slow grinding voice went on. 'Course I don't know if you're dead yet, but you will be soon, you bastard. You think I didn't know who you were soon's I saw you? Ain't nobody I forgit once I seen 'em. You was next on my list back there in the Dakota country, you better believe it. You shoulda seen them two marshals when I finished with 'em, whoo, man. One of 'em had a serpent-dæmon and he took his eyes off me and I picked her up by the tail and cracked her like a goddamn whip. You ain't never seen a man so surprised to be dead. That was by the Cheyenne River. And it left the other man on his own against Pierre McConville. That ain't good odds, Scoresby, you think of that. I can stay awake longer'n anyone. He tried to out-wake me but in the end he fell into the sweet arms of slumber, and the sucker thought he'd tied me safe, but ain't nothing can hold me down. I got a trick for that. I snuck out of my bonds and I lashed that son of a whore's feet and hands together and then I just picked up his dæmon and tied her to his horse and unhobbled the horse. Man! That was funny. He woke up and he saw the terrible fix he was in. He kept saying, "Here, Sunshine, good horse, don't go 'way now, come on, you dumb critter, please please now don't move." As long as that horse didn't move too far he could just about live, but if something was to startle her so she ran off, well, bang, thassit. Like a hand coming up inside your ribs and feeling your heart still beating and pulling and pulling it till the strings and the veins all pop and it comes away in your hand. Man, you're dead then all right. In the end I took his gun and I fired it in the air and off ol' Sunshine took like a cannon ball. You ain't never heard a scream like that marshal screamed.

'Well, I'm gone do that to you, Scoresby. There's that big hoist outside the doors there with a rope on it. I'm gone play a trick with that, you bet. I'm gone play with you and that scrawny jackrabbit for a *long* time.'

The pool of fish oil had spread. It was close enough now for Lee to reach out and touch it, and then he saw Hester look that way too, and then at him, and then at his pistol, and he knew at once what she meant.

McConville was still talking, but Lee blanked out his voice and with infinite care reached for the pistol at his waist. Holding it on his lap, he touched a finger to the pool of oil and brought a drop to the pivot of the hammer, and another to the trigger mechanism, and another to the bearing of the cylinder. With his weakened left hand holding the barrel as firmly as he could, he turned the cylinder with his right, very slowly, and felt it loosen. He pulled back the hammer: it moved stiffly at first, and then freely. He made sure there was a cartridge in the chamber, and sat with the pistol cocked, waiting for McConville's deep grating voice to stop.

'Well, Scoresby, I'm gone start killing you now. This

is your end a-coming. It's gone be a hard one and a long one. I made that other marshal's end last a good half-hour by his pretty watch, which I took. I think I might let you stick around a mite longer'n that. Depends how much you scream.'

Lee heard the sound of a man getting to his feet and coughing slightly as if to cover a grunt of pain. So he had been hit!

And Hester pricked up her ears, tensing suddenly, as she and Lee heard another sound: the slither of a serpent body along a wooden floor, and the faint dry clicking of a rattle. McConville's dæmon, impatient to get the torture started, was moving ahead of him.

And then, not six feet away at the end of the rack of barrels, the snake-head appeared – and Hester sprang, and seized it.

She gripped the dæmon just behind the head, and bit down hard. Lee felt every quiver of her muscles, and clenched his teeth in sympathy with hers.

McConville uttered a great cry of rage and pain and fell to the floor behind the barrels. Unable to move, Lee watched the furious struggle between the lashing, coiling, whipping snake and the tense little form of Hester, her claws slipping as she scrabbled on the floor. There was nothing for her to get any purchase on – no good turf, no springy twigs of sage – nothing but smooth boards, and the little rabbit had only half the weight of the snake; and Lee could feel with his dæmon the furious power of the twisting, writhing form of McConville's as she flung herself left, right, left, trying to tear her neck out from between Hester's teeth.

'Keep going, gal,' Lee whispered. 'Hold tight there, sweetheart…'

And she dug in, she tightened her trembling jaw, she scrabbled and slipped but she dug in again and tugged, and dragged, and hauled, and little by little pulled McConville's dæmon away from him.

McConville's cries were hideous. He scrambled across the floor – Lee could hear his boots slipping, his fingernails scratching – his grunts and roars echoed around the warehouse till the air was full of the noise, and then helplessly he stumbled round the end of the rack of barrels, and Lee shot him.

McConville crashed backwards against the window and slid to the floor. In Hester's mouth his dæmon sagged and loosened, but Hester kept on tugging, and it was easier now, and McConville sobbed, 'No – no – don't do it – goddamn bitch rabbit –'

His face was the colour of dirty paper. His mouth was a sagging red hole and his eyes were bulging.

'McConville,' said Lee, 'you shot Mike Martinez and Broadus Vinson from a hiding place, like a coward, and then you made little Jimmy Partlett fight you because he didn't want you to think he was a coward. You're a dirty piece of work, and this is the end of you.'

And he shot the man through the heart. His dæmon vanished, and Hester tumbled back towards Lee, who scooped her up and kissed her and held her close till she stopped trembling.

'You better move, Lee,' she whispered. 'You got about ten seconds before you're sitting in a pool of fish oil.'

'And now our troubles begin, Hester,' Lee muttered, struggling to pull himself upright, and just in time, too.

Gingerly he moved his left arm and found, at least, that he could. He put his pistol back in the holster and went to pick up the rifle.

Then he looked out of the window and saw the ship's crew at work covering the forward hatch, so they must have loaded the cargo. But one man lay dead on the deck, under a sheet of canvas, and nearby on the quay a crowd headed by Poliakov was being held at bay by Iorek Byrnison, whose bulk stood foursquare on the flagstones confronting them. Poliakov was addressing the crowd; Lee could hear the muscular drone of his voice, but not the words. He was trying to get them to move forward and – well, attack the schooner, Lee supposed, but the bear would have stopped a madder, braver crowd than this.

Lee could also hear the chug of the schooner's auxiliary engine, and see the exhaust smoke puffing from the pipe amidships. She was nearly ready to leave.

He made his way carefully down the stairs. On the ground floor he found a chaos of torn bundles of skins, broken spars and lengths of timber, and the great steel sheet of the door lying flat beside the entrance.

He walked out into the sunlight and made his way to the bear's side.

'Well, Iorek Byrnison, the trouble's gone from upstairs,' he said.

The bear's head swung round to look at him, the black eyes glinting under the great iron ridge.

And then Lee's head swam and he lost his balance for a moment, but the bear's head moved in a flash and seized his coat between his teeth, and gently pulled him upright again.

And then things became confusing.

There was someone shouting from the crowd, or did it come from beyond them? Loud voices bellowing commands, anyway, and then the disciplined quick tramp-tramp-tramp of running feet in heavy boots coming along the quay. Behind him, Lee heard a splash, and then turned carefully to see the bear's helmeted head emerging from the water and moving swiftly away.

But he had to turn round again, because an angry voice was shouting, 'You! Drop your weapon! Drop it now!'

And he saw it came from the man in charge of the squad of running men in Larsen Manganese uniforms, who had arrived at the head of the crowd now and stood, rifles aimed, facing him like a firing squad. Poliakov was standing safely behind them, frowning his approval.

Lee considered that he didn't feel inclined to drop that nice rifle, and he was about to say so when another layer of confusion was added to the mix. A different voice from behind him said, 'Mr Lee Scoresby, you are under arrest.'

Cautiously, in case he fell over, Lee turned once more. The man who'd spoken was one of three; young, armed with a pistol, and in a different uniform.

'Who the hell are you?' Lee said.

'Never mind him!' yelled the Larsen Manganese leader. 'Do as I say!'

'I am Lieutenant Haugland. We are from the Customs and Revenue Board, Mr Scoresby,' said the young man calmly, 'and I repeat, you are under arrest. Put down your rifle.'

'Well, you see,' said Lee, 'if I do that, the Senator over there will suddenly regain his courage, and order those marionettes of his to come and take over Captain van Breda's ship. And after all me and York Byrnison went through to help him load his cargo, that seems kind of a pity. I don't know how to resolve this situation, Mr Customs Officer.'

'I will resolve it. Put your rifle down, please.'

The young officer stepped past Lee and faced the line of riflemen without a tremor.

'You will all leave the harbour now, and go about your lawful business,' he said, loudly enough for everyone to hear. 'If there is one person left on this quayside by the time the Customs House clock strikes twelve, they will be arrested. All of you move.'

The Larsen Manganese men looked uncertain. But Poliakov, still taking care to remain behind them, shouted:

'I protest! This is an outrage! I am the leader of a properly constituted political party, and this is a blatant attempt to deny my freedom of speech! You should be enforcing the law, not flouting it! That criminal Scoresby –'

'Mr Scoresby is under arrest, and so will you be if you do not turn round and leave the harbour. You have two minutes.'

Lieutenant Haugland's fox-dæmon said something quietly to Hester. Poliakov drew himself up to his full height, and gave in.

'Very well,' he said. 'Under strong protest, and cheated of the justice we have a right to expect and a duty to demand, we shall do as you say. But I give you notice that –'

'Less than two minutes,' said Haugland.

Poliakov turned, and the crowd behind parted to let him through, and sullenly followed him away. The Larsen Manganese riflemen were the last to turn, but the implacable stillness of the Customs officer outfaced them, and finally their leader muttered an order, and they turned and walked back down the quay – walked, until he snapped another order and they clumsily organised themselves into a march.

'Mr Scoresby, your rifle, if you please,' said the young man.

'I would rather give it back to Captain van Breda,' Lee said, 'seeing that it belongs to him.'

He heard hasty footsteps behind him, and turned

carefully again to see the Captain hurrying towards them. He had evidently heard the last exchange, because he said:

'Mr Scoresby, I must thank you – I have nothing to pay you with except the rifle itself – please take it, please. It is yours.'

'Very handsome, Captain,' said Lee. 'I'll accept it with thanks.'

'And now put it down,' said Haugland.

Lee bent to lay it on the ground.

'And your pistol.'

'It doesn't work,' said Lee.

'Yes it does. Put it down.'

Lee did so, and then straightened up, feeling dizzy. For a moment the sounds of the harbour receded: the cry of the gulls, the raised voices from the coal tanker and the crane driver across the water, the splash of the dredger, the striking of the Customs House clock; and then it seemed as if a dark cloud had sprung up out of nowhere and enveloped the sun, because the colour drained from the world and everything dimmed.

It only lasted a moment, and then he found another officer's hand steadying his arm, and came to his full senses again.

'Follow me, please,' said the officer, and set off briskly towards the end of the quay. As Lee passed the schooner he could see the crew unseating the heel of the derrick, and a man casting off a rope, and Captain van Breda hurrying up the gangplank and shouting an order.

'Where are we going?' said Lee. 'I thought your Customs House was back there.'

'It is,' said the Lieutenant, and left it at that; but as they passed the last warehouse Lee saw a launch tied up at a flight of steps, in the Customs and Revenue colours of navy and white. The engine was chugging quietly, and a rating held the painter tight through a ring in the wall to keep the boat steady as the first officer stepped on board.

Lee crouched to pick up Hester, who whispered, 'It's all right, Lee. Everything's fine.'

Deeply puzzled, he stepped on to the launch, and sat down in the little cabin as the other two officers followed.

The sailor cast off, and one of the officers took the wheel and opened the throttle. Lee looked back at the schooner, whose bow was already swinging out away from the quay.

The young officer had laid Lee's pistol and the Winchester on the bench opposite where Lee was sitting, and Lee could easily have reached either of them. He sat still and quiet, holding Hester close, until the launch had passed the dredger and rounded the lighthouse, and was pitching briskly in the waves of the open sea.

'All right, I give up,' he said. 'What the hell is going on?'

'Mr Scoresby, please take your pistol,' said Haugland. 'And I believe the rifle is also yours.'

'Well, now I'm dreaming,' said Lee. He took

the revolver and spun the cylinder, which ran smoothly and surely. 'Where are we going, and why?'

'We are going round the headland to the Barents Sea Company Depot, where you will find your balloon inflated and ready to leave. Here, by the way, is your luggage from the boarding house.'

He took Lee's kitbag from a locker. Too numb to be surprised any longer, Lee nodded and took it silently.

The officer at the wheel changed course, and the boat pitched and rolled in the lively sea. Lee watched the rocky shoreline, and saw a seal surface, and then another and another.

'They are fleeing from the bear,' said Haugland.

'Where's he?'

'On his way to the depot. He is not interested in seals for now. He has something to give you.'

'Well, this is a damn surprising morning,' said Lee.

'The fact is this, Mr Scoresby: there is a struggle going on throughout the northern lands, of which this little island is a microcosm. On one hand there are the properly constituted civil institutions such as the Customs and Revenue Board, and on the other the uncontrolled power of the large private companies such as Larsen Manganese, which are dominating more and more of public life, though they are not subject to any form of democratic sanction. If Mr Poliakov wins this election, he will make life easier for Larsen Manganese and its fellows, and worse for the people of Novy Odense.'

'I thought he was campaigning against the bears,' said Lee. 'I thought that was his whole platform.'

'That is what he wants simple people to think.'

'Oh,' said Lee. 'Simple people, eh. Well, he certainly worked that trick.'

'Until now he has been very careful to remain just within the law, but trying to deprive Captain van Breda of that cargo was a step too far. Whoever hired those gunmen was also, of course, committing a crime, but I have no doubt that we shall find it impossible to prove any connection with Poliakov. I am also sure that his lawyers will manage to confuse the court and secure an acquittal in the matter of the cargo. In short, Mr Scoresby, we are grateful to you for dealing with an unpleasant problem. Your action was all the more honourable in that you had no personal interest in the matter.'

'Oh, I don't think much about honour,' Lee said uncomfortably.

'Well, we are grateful, as I say. You will find your balloon fully provisioned, and there is a good east wind.'

Lee looked ahead through the spray-splashed cabin window. They were rapidly approaching the mole sheltering the depot, and Lee could see his balloon, as the young man had promised, already inflated and swaying in the wind. It was a case of thank you very much and don't come back, he thought.

As the launch passed the mole and slowed down in the calmer water inside it, Lee felt gingerly inside his coat for the damage to his shoulder. It hurt like hell, but as far as he could tell it hadn't done any structural damage. As for his ear, he felt that too; there was a bite-shaped gap at the top big enough to fit a finger in, and it was still bleeding.

'Before you put me in my balloon and cut the tether and wave goodbye,' he said, 'is there somewhere I can fix myself up? I take it you have no objection if I patch up the holes I seem to have acquired?'

'No objection whatsoever,' said Haugland drily.

The officer at the wheel cut the throttle and the launch drifted neatly to a halt beside a wooden jetty. A moment later it was secured, and Lee stood up to follow the Customs men ashore.

There was a huddle of low buildings around the Company offices, and they took Lee first to sign for the return of his balloon. The clerk looked at him without surprise.

'You found someone to fight with, then,' he said.

Lee saw that the storage fee had already been paid, and so had the bill for the gas. He pushed the release form back across the counter without a word; the fact was that he could think of nothing to say.

'This way, Mr Scoresby,' said the Lieutenant.

He led Lee to a washroom, where Lee painfully stripped to the waist, cleaned himself as best he could, and with Hester's help examined the damage. He was glad to see that McConville's bullet had gone through the muscle of his shoulder and out again; it might have clipped the bone on the way, but at least he wouldn't have to dig the damn thing out. As for his ear, that was too bad. He could still hear with it.

'Wasn't all that pretty anyway,' said Hester.

'Prettiest one I had,' said Lee.

The officer knocked on the door. 'Mr Scoresby,' he called, 'there is a medical man here who will look at you.'

Lee opened the door, shivering in the brisk wind, and found Lieutenant Haugland, smiling, standing on the cinder path next to Iorek Byrnison.

The bear was carrying a bundle of dark green in his mouth, which he dropped into the officer's hands.

'Bloodmoss,' he said. 'Let me see your wounds.'

'A truly remarkable specific,' said the officer, as Lee turned to show the bear his shoulder. 'It has antiseptic and analgesic properties superior to anything in our hospitals.'

Iorek took a few strands of the moss, and chewed them briefly. He dropped the pounded mess into Lee's right hand.

'Lay it in the wound and bind it up,' he said. 'It will heal quickly.'

'Well, thank you kindly, York Byrnison,' said Lee. 'I appreciate that.'

He did his best with the soggy moss. The Lieutenant tore off a strip of adhesive tape and bound the wound for him, and Lee pulled his shirt on again.

While his head was still inside it, he heard quick footsteps on the path, and another man's voice: one he recognised. He held still a moment to think what to do, and then he pulled the shirt down to see the dark-suited figure of the poet and journalist Oskar Sigurdsson, notebook in hand, talking eagerly to the Lieutenant.

'...and it occurred to me that – Ah! The hero himself! Mr Scoresby, I congratulate you on your safe escape! Would it be too much trouble to ask you for an interview about this remarkable episode?'

Lee looked around. The jetty was only a few yards away.

He said, 'Why, certainly, Mr Sigurdsson, but I think we need a little privacy. Come with me.'

He led the way out, and Sigurdsson followed eagerly. When they were at the end of the jetty, Lee pointed out to sea.

'You see that spot on the horizon? Might be a ship?'

Sigurdsson peered, sheltering his eyes.

'I think so –' he began, but he got no further, because Lee stepped behind him and swung his foot hard against the poet's backside. With a cry of alarm Sigurdsson shot forward and into the sea, arms flailing.

Lee walked back to the washroom and said, 'Mr Sigurdsson seems to have fallen into the water. He might need a hand to get out. I'd oblige myself, but unfortunately I'm indisposed.'

'I think it is lucky for us that you are leaving, Mr Scoresby,' said Haugland. 'Petersen! Bring him ashore and wring him out, if you would.'

Another man ran to the end of the jetty with a lifebelt, but before Lee could see Sigurdsson rescued, there was the sound of yet more footsteps, and in a hurry this time; and as Lee was pulling on his coat, around the corner of the buildings came another of his acquaintances.

'Mr Vassiliev!' Lee said. 'You come to say goodbye?'

The economist was out of breath, and his eyes were wide with anxiety.

'They are coming this way – the Larsen security men – they have orders to kill you and the bear – Poliakov is furious –'

Iorek Byrnison growled and turned to the sea, but Vassiliev went on:

'They have a gunboat on its way too. There's no way out.'

'There's one way,' said Lee. 'You ever flown in a balloon, York Byrnison?'

'Iorek,' growled the bear. 'No, Mr Scarsby, I have not.'

'Iorek. Got it. And I'm Scoresby, but make it Lee. Well, now's the time, Iorek. Mr Vassiliev, good day, and thanks.'

He shook hands with the economist, and the officer accompanied Lee and the bear to the balloon, which was shivering with impatience to be free of its tether and take to the sky. Lee checked everything: it was all in good order.

'Go,' said Haugland, and shook his hand. 'Oh – take your rifle.'

He handed Lee the Winchester, which Lee took with pleasure; he felt as if it had been made for him. He wrapped it in oilcloth before stowing it carefully inside the gondola.

'You ready, Iorek?' he said.

'This is strange to me,' said the bear. 'But I will trust you. You are a man of the Arctic.'

'I am? How's that?'

'Your dæmon is an Arctic hare.'

'A *what*?' said Hester. 'I thought I was a damn jackrabbit!'

'Arctic hare,' said Iorek briefly, and Haugland nodded.

Lee was as amazed as she was, but there wasn't time to stop and discuss the matter. Iorek clambered over the side into the capacious gondola, having tested the strength of it to his own satisfaction, and then Lee joined him.

'Lieutenant Haugland, I'm obliged to you, sir,' he said. 'But I still don't see how you knew who I was, and where I was boarding.'

'You may thank Miss Victoria Lund,' the Lieutenant continued, 'to whom, as of this morning, I have the honour to be engaged. She told me that you had been very courteous towards her.'

Lee tugged off his hat and scratched his head,

and then rammed his hat on again and tugged it low, because he was blushing.

'Please – ah – convey my respects to Miss Lund,' he mumbled. 'I congratulate you on your engagement, sir. Miss Lund is a remarkable young lady.'

He dared not look at Hester.

'Hmm,' he went on. 'Well, let's get away. Iorek, if I need two hands, you might have to help me out a little till that bloodmoss kicks in. Stand clear now!'

He released the tether, and the balloon sprang upwards with the swift assurance of a craft that knew where it was going and was eager to get there. It felt like a living thing. Lee loved that first rush of speed, and so did Hester.

He checked all his instruments, and looked around the sky, and then looked down at the rapidly diminishing scene below. With the help of his field glasses Lee made out a little shivering figure wrapped in blankets on the jetty. Along the road from the town a convoy of armoured cars was moving towards the depot, and from further down the coast a gunboat was speeding in the same direction with a great deal of flashy spray.

Further away, he could see the schooner just

passing the lighthouse. The crew had raised the sails, and the ship was catching the strong east wind that was speeding the balloon on its way.

Iorek was crouching low on the floor of the basket, keeping absolutely still. At first Lee thought he was asleep, but then he realised that the great bear was afraid.

'You reckon young Lieutenant Haugland will deal with those Larsen Manganese bullies?' Lee said, to distract him; he had no doubt himself.

'Yes. I have a high regard for him.'

Lee thought that the bear's high regard would be a thing worth having.

Hester moved along the floor, closer to the bear's head, and settled down to speak to him quietly. Lee left her to it, and checked the barometer, the gas-pressure gauge and the compass again, not that the compass was much of a help in these latitudes; and then he took out the rifle, looked it over thoroughly, cleaned it and oiled it with a new can of machine oil, which he found to his surprise in the tool box. He wrapped it up again carefully before making sure it was safely strapped to a stanchion. He'd learnt his lesson; he looked after it well for the rest of his life, and thirty-five years later, the Winchester was in his hands when he died.

Looking around his unnaturally tidy gondola, he discovered some neatly wrapped packets in the starboard locker, and opened one to find some rye crispbread and hard cheese. He also discovered that he was very hungry.

Some time later, when they were high in the blue sky and everything was well, Lee opened his kitbag to take out his warm waistcoat. His clothes were more neatly folded than they had ever been, and there was a sprig of lavender on the top.

'Well, Hester,' he said, 'this has been a surprising day, and no mistake. How's Iorek over there?'

'Asleep,' she said. 'What's surprising? You acting the fool and kissing that lavender ain't surprising.'

'No, I don't reckon that is. I could lose my heart to that girl. Flying with a bear, now – that's surprising.'

'More surprising if you left him there. You wouldn't do that. If we couldn't take him, we'd stand and fight beside him.'

'Well, all right then. Finding out that you're an Arctic hare – that's surprising. Damn, I was surprised.'

'Surprised? Why the hell were you surprised? I ain't surprised,' said Hester. 'Iorek's right. I always knew I had more class than a rabbit.'

THE END

NOVOROSSISK, Russia. Lat. 60° 47′ N; long. 21° 24′ E.
                    A rising port on the Caucasian coast of the Black Sea,
about 400 miles distant from Odessa, and 200 from Batoum. **Pop.** 40,000. **Tr.–** I.
Machinery, general; E. Grain, seed, oilcake, kerosene, oak staves. It is connected
with the general network of Russian railway by a branch line to Tichoretskai
on the Wladikavkaz. Rail to Petrovsk and Baku; thus the Captain and Black
Sea are in direct communication. The Railway Co.'s elevator is stated to be the
largest in the world. **Accn.** There are 7 loading piers, of which 5 (including
2 elevator piers) belong to the Railway Co., 1 to the French Standard Oil Co.,
and 1 to the Russian Steamship Co., hence there is accommodation for some 22
steamers. The depth of water at the ends of these piers averages about 24 to
26ft. There are two breakwaters. Cranes to 5, 10, and 20 tons, floating crane
to 40 tons, elevator capacity 3,000,000 poods. **Charges.** Harb dues, Custom
House charges, loading and discharging expenses: – The Rly. Co. exacts from
steamers 10 copecs per net reg. ton for the use of its piers, and for merchants
_ to 1_ copecs per pood of cargo loaded or discharged, for use of the wagons,
labourers, &c. Custom House dues, 20 copecs per net reg. ton on steamers. No
pilots. Discharging, general, about 50 cop. per ton. **Officials.** British Vice-
Consul, A. Geelmuyden; Lloyd's Agent, ——.

NOVY ODENSE, Muscovy. Lat. 64° 34′ N; long. 40° 32′ E.
                    (On Is. of the same name). Railway to Barents Sea
Company Depot. **Pop.** 12,000. **THW.** Varies. About 1hr later each day. **Tr.**
– I. Coal, salt, hardware, machinery, timber, sugar, grain, meats frozen and
preserved, coffee, wines, spirits, canvas, cordage, etc; E. fish-oil, seal-oil, rock-oil,
preserved fish, skins, furs. **Accn.** There is a good harb. and vessels drawing 17 to
18 ft can lie alongside the quays. The channel has a depth of 19ft, and there are
21ft of water on the bar. Vessels drawing up to 18ft must cross bar and shoal in
two tides; vessels of 17ft and less may enter in one tide. Dredging continually
all summer. Good sheds alongside East quay, sheds and rails along West quay.
One steam crane on **W.** quay, 20 tons, and two anbaric cranes on **E.**, 12 and 8
tons. **Charges.** Tonnage dues, 20 copecks per reg. ton. Customs most strict about
declaration of goods, stores, &c, landing without permit, or concealment. Sailing
vessels discharging solid ballast, 40 copecks per ton. **Pilotage.** Harb. pilotage is
not compulsory, but if a pilot be required the usual charge is 6 copecks per reg.
ton in, and 6 copecks out. Towage. 36 to 80 roubles from port to sea, ships and
steamers. **Coaling, &c.** Coal, ground-gas, rock-oil available at Barents Sea
Company Depot, 2 miles SSW (2 jetties, good anchorage close to shore in 15 to
20 fms. Vessels drawing over 15 ft are discharged and loaded by lighters, which
in their turn are discharged and loaded alongside moles). **Officials.** Harbour-
Master, J. Aagaard; Commissioner of Customs, K. Hagström; British Consul-
General, W.R.K. Ward; Lloyd's Agent, A. Deacon. **Broker.** I.A. Denisov.

NYBORG,Denmark.
                    At the head of a fjord about 3 miles long, branching off the
Great Belt. **Pop.** 8,000. **Tr.–** I. Grain, cotton seed, oil cakes, sunflower oil cakes,
bran, coal, cakes, timber; E. Barley, butter, pork, bacon, cattle. **Accn.** Old East harb.
has **D.** of 18_ ft; **Charges.** Harb. dues in and out 20 ore ton, or 10 ore each way,
loaded or in ballast; ballast, 85 ore ton; ballast dues, 2 ore per ton reg. **Pilotage.**
After tariff rates. **Officials.** British Vice-Consul, A. Birch; Lloyd's Agent, R. O. Clausen.

SHOCKING AFFAIR AT HARBOUR.

TWO MEN SLAIN IN WAREHOUSE SHOOTING.

VILLAIN AND ACCOMPLICE BEAR FLEE BY BALLOON.

By our Special Correspondent Oskar Sigurdsson.

Two trusted employees of the Larsen Manganese Company were mercilessly slaughtered yesterday in the course of their duty, and two others were grievously wounded.

The affair took place in the peaceful surroundings of the harbour, where a vessel had been held up for some days following the refusal of its captain to pay the storage fees due on a cargo he claimed he had the right to load.

It appears that the captain, van Breden by name, engaged the assassin to achieve by force what his own obstinacy had failed to bring about.

The perpetrator of this appalling crime appears to be a foreigner, one Leigh Scroby, a Texan, who came to our town by balloon. He is evidently a cold-blooded and calculating killer. Your correspondent had a brief interview with him on the evening before the tragic events at the harbour, and it was clear even in the civilized surroundings of our Town Hall that here was a man whose deceitful and violent nature made him unfit company for those of a peace-loving disposition. He openly carried a pistol, and one, furthermore, which was well-tended and ready for action.

What makes this crime even more shocking in the eyes of decent citizens is that the murderer was joined in his dastardly action by a bear. This savage brute, degraded even by the low standards of his race, had evidently conspired with Scroby beforehand to carry out the atrocious deed.

The two villains fled the scene of their crime together, aided (one is sorry to say) by the interference of the Customs authorities, whose high-handed officer, in placing legalistic correctness before anything else, prevented the swift and stern application of natural justice.

Those with a shrewd understanding of political matters will find in all the circumstances of this tragic affair further proof, if proof be needed, of the far-sighted wisdom of Ivan Dimitrovich Poliakov, the leading candidate for Mayor in the forthcoming election.

Mr Poliakov writes in the current edition of the *Novy Odense Courier and Telegraph* **(p.7).**

18 October

Dear Tom,

It's going to have to be Econ Hist because there simply isn't any way of examining what I know about the alethiometer. Ideally there'd be a panel of wise men and women who could test me on it and judge the merits of a thesis and so on but there's only me and Dame H, and I'm beginning to get beyond the things she knows about anyway. I'll have to keep on with that privately and — well, privately. At least with Econ Hist the body of knowledge is nice and clear and I've got a really good subject and lots of documents and stuff (personal knowledge etc) and if I get all the postgrad qualifications I can teach it and earn a living. So how does this sound as a title for my dissertation? 'Patterns of trade in the Arctic region with particular reference to independent cargo balloon carriage (1950-1970).'

It must be a winner.

Yours

L

ST SOPHIA'S COLLEGE, Oxford

Tuesday 2nd January

Dear Dr Polstead,

Sorry to bother you with this, but I wonder if you could advise me about a small point. I've got a number of items of printed matter to enter into the bibliography for my dissertation – some of them are scraps, really, not much more than ~~ephemara~~ ephemera, but they all build up a picture – and the thing I need to know is how to enter them correctly if they aren't obvious things like books. Also, when the item I'm referring to in the text is (for example) a cutting from a newspaper that isn't going to be available anywhere in Oxford, or England for that matter, and so won't be easy for the examiners to check, would it be necessary to provide the actual cutting? I could do that easily enough. Some of my bits and pieces are precious for personal reasons, but I daresay the examiners will be careful to return them intact.

With thanks

Yours

Lyra

CERTIFICATE FOR DISSERTATIONS
SUBMITTED IN MASTERS' COURSES IN
THE FACULTY OF HISTORY.

This certificate should be placed in a sealed envelope, bearing on
the outside your candidate's number only, addressed to the Chairman
of Examiners, and it should be taken by hand to the Examination
Schools in the High Street and left in the designated receptacle.

Candidate number: *23*

Name: *Lyra Silvertongue*

College: *St Sophia's*

Title of masters' programme: *M. Phil in Economic History*

Title of dissertation: *Developments in patterns of trade in the
European Arctic region with particular reference to
independent cargo balloon carriage (1950-1970)*

Number of words used: *28,950*

I declare the following:

1. The dissertation I am submitting is entirely my own work, unless
   otherwise indicated by citation or quotation
2. No substantial portion of it has been presented for any other
   degree course or examination
3. It does not exceed the prescribed work limit for the degree
   including footnotes, excluding bibliography, any appendices for
   which specific permission has been obtained, and any English
   translations of passages quoted in another language

Candidate's signature: *Lyra Silvertongue*